The Story of a
Small Life

BY B. J. CHUTE

B. J. CHUTE

The Story of a Small Life

E. P. DUTTON & CO., INC.   NEW YORK   1971

Fourth Printing, May 1972

Published simultaneously in Canada
by Clarke, Irwin & Company Limited, Toronto and Vancouver

Library of Congress Catalog Card Number: 70-165597
SBN 0-525-21108-4

to the City of New York
with astonishment and respect

. . . rejoice not that the spirits are
subject unto you, but rather rejoice because
your names are written in heaven.
Luke 10:20

1

Richard Harris
Richard Harris
Richard Harris
as if I could make myself known to myself this way by writing
my own name over and over

This is a warm-up, like typing "The quick brown fox jumps
over the lazy dog." I haven't been this sorry for myself in a long
time, and it can be explained, clinically and briskly, as the
product of a twelve-hour day, filled with an excessive amount
of meanness and dirt and grubbing in the interests of the Underprivileged, the Disadvantaged, the Deprived or whatever
culturally acceptable euphemism is in current use. They can
also be called the seedy, the lazy, the damned, the buoyant, the
vicious, the crippled and the beautiful.

I could quit this job if I wanted to, of course. No one has
locked me into it except myself, since I only took it to study
Humanity, make a buck and still have time to write. It was all
labeled opportunity by the University in the sharp-nosed, flat-
cheeked person of Professor Blount, although in retrospect I
am ready to believe that he was only saving me from Graduate
School where I would certainly have curled up like a worm in
a tepid cocoon. Blount was a tougher and more croaking
monster than I took him to be at the time; all that he was

9

really saying was "Get out of my sight, boy, and keep yourself occupied. Either you'll write, or you won't." O Thalia, Calliope and Melpomene, I had everything in those days, including just enough back trouble to keep me out of the Army trap and just enough talent to make me believe that I was an artist. Not to mention the modest conviction that I knew the world as man had never known it before.

Subsequently, of course, I decided that I was born too soon, into an undergraduate twilight where no one raised a hand against a professor except to ask a question. I was anterior to all the campus riots, but there is a part of me that would have loved to have been there in the grunting fraternal dark. A part of me has always gone about, striding up and down, manning the barricades and chanting the Marseillaise. I think now that I would have enjoyed those days, but I once thought the same thing about this job, into which I fell so conveniently. This well-paid and idealistic job, funded philanthropically (when did the giants of the earth acquire names like Ford and Rocke-feller and U.S. Treasury?) and conceived generously for the betterment of mankind. They needed college graduates who only asked to serve, and I needed an operation which would keep me eating, justify my existence on earth and help me garner material for that first great novel.

Which is now in a suitcase at the back of my only closet, unsold, unsung. No one wanted it when I finished it, and no one wants it now. Only Jeannie thought that it was a great book, becoming a little more totally loyal with each rejection. Jeannie was my high-hearted girl, with thick legs. She would walk on any picket line, join any movement and lie in any bed.

The suitcase contains other artifacts, of course, in the form of short stories whose only distinction was that they came back faster than the novel. It takes time for a novel to trundle around an editorial office, no doubt. Someone must give an impression of having scuffled through all those neat pages, adding a thumbprint here, a blot of coffee there, for honesty's sake. But a short story now, any fool can scan twenty pages and send it back within the hour. No one need ever know except the expanding Post Office and the shriveling artist.

I haven't written a short story in months, nothing with any shape, just five-finger exercises sacred to the memory of Professor Blount. Am I still reluctant to disappoint him? Good. He expects me to produce, pointing his finger at my typewriter, keeping an eye on my sidling thoughts. "Write what you know," he used to say inevitably, but I know so much now that I know nothing and I am sick of it anyway and would very much like to be able to retreat and to find, perhaps at the very center, an object recognizable as my Self and about which I could write. So I type my name three times at the top of a page, and instead of invoking my Self I exorcise it and become one of those Chinese dragons that chew their own tails. Probably the price you pay for living other people's lives all day long is that you never live your own at all.

I don't believe that. Begin again.

I take a very narrow view of these streets, this small section of New York for which I have a certain (chronic and funded) responsibility. I have become very good at prescribing for trouble just before it erupts, satisfying needs before they get so bloated that they cannot be suppressed. Good at suppressing, cajoling, good at ferreting out the law and at laying it down. I know the symptoms of drug addiction, the degraded but somehow horribly comforted eye of the "stoned" (like a martyr? like St. Stephen?) and the slippery candid eye of the pusher. I know the swelling bellies of fifteen-year-old girls, and I know the kids who will plant the harvest they will bear. Some of them are nasty little creeps, and some of them are as decent as little dogs and just as ignorant.

I knew them all in my novel, even before I met any of them, and I set them down on paper but I set them down inadequately. Now, when I know I could write them better, I would

11

rather not even think about them. I want to think about something else but I don't know what the something else is, and, if I could find it, perhaps I could leave this job and this street and be free of all of them—the depraved and the decent, from the drug-pusher who is wholly a snake, to that black giantess who is raising five children in two rooms with a kind of bellowing fury and the monstrous joy that I once felt when I was five years old and lay flat on my back in a sludge of mud and yelled straight up at the sun.

I could leave her. She would not miss me or change in any particular, any more than all the others would. Richard Harris, informer, prop, perpetual source of small loans that are not meant to be paid back, soothsayer, friend, enemy, soft palm in a hard-knuckle world.

I could walk out on them. I think I could walk out on them tomorrow, except for Mig who is becoming a sort of obsession with me. He is so clever and so stupid. At seventeen, he could be anything he wants to be, but he has chosen to be the bored king of a narrow street, handling his bright knife of cleverness which will probably some day slit his own thin throat, listening to me with his dark-eyed respectful look and then sliding past my words with his mean, self-satisfied grace. I have twice kept him out of jail (jail is no answer at all) and I have turned my head away ten times as often, so as not to see what he was doing, because I still think that I am God and that I can certainly save this one life out of so many. Saving, at the same time, the life of that round-faced, helpless, forlorn child named Anna, who should be safe at home with her family in Brooklyn and whom he treats like a cheap toy.

If I go away, there is going to be one piece of trouble here that will be one too much, and, if I stay, it is just possible that something might be different. If I could affect Mig's life, in the name of the Father, the Son and the Foundation, wouldn't I have a right to feel that I had done something, and not done it too badly?

2

No one was going to affect Mig's life. Neither Richard Harris nor Anna nor Father Bailey nor anyone else.

He had been born knowing that he was in a jungle, so life had already provided him with an excuse for treating it in whatever way he wished. He was small king of his streets, and he planned to be king of a great deal more, but he had never joined with any gang since the one thing he had was his own cleverness, and that he would not share. His name was not Mig. He had chosen a new name the day he left home, and he had never gone back to his mother and his two sisters, who had seemed to be running away all the time, away from nothing and toward nothing. He was not going to run with them, scraping for food, scratching for rent, whining for welfare services, praying to saints who gave no relief and crying sentimentally toward their son and brother to be a man and to regain that lost Heaven which somebody, somewhere, owed to them.

He was hard and sharp, and one day he simply walked out the door, not even leaving a scratch of his bad writing on paper as a good-bye. He chose a new set of streets, out of reach, and he gave himself a new name, calling himself after the fighter planes which he thought meant absolute freedom. On the street of his careless choice, he quickly found that Mig was accepted as being short for Miguel. But he was not Spanish, not Puerto Rican, not black, not white. He seemed to have a touch of everything, that perfect ethnic mixture that can vanish in anonymity, and, by the time they knew him well on his new streets, they knew he was Mig for a fighter plane and not Mig for Miguel.

He had not brought Anna to this new world with him, but she had followed. Somehow, she had found out where he was and had come, calling him by his real name (pious Joseph, after some hand-washing saint; baptized Joseph but born Mig), turning up suddenly at his side, putting her hand into his, and never telling him how she had known where to find him. She was an arousing mixture to him of child and girl and woman; for his vanity's sake, he found he could not quite do without her. He let her stay on condition that she would not call him Joseph and that she would accept what he did without question.

He was seventeen, and Anna was certainly not his first. He took her as his easy right and used her precisely as he wished to, and all that first night she had kept her face turned to the wall. But he was very well content with himself, and she was a silent girl anyway, even more silent now that she had left her mother behind her. Her mother would, quite probably, have killed him. It was one of the many things he chose not to think about, having two wishes: not to be dead, and not to go to jail. To avoid the first, he stayed away from Anna's mother and a few enemy knives. To avoid the second, he had needed only to find a man named Richard Harris and to exercise on him knowingly the winelike sweetness and charm that were peculiarly his own.

As to money, there were ways of making it, and all of them irresistible. The best was Richard Harris, and the Foundation behind him. (Mig pictured it square and white and blank-faced like a bank.) Mr. Harris listened to Mig attentively and saw him, like his mother and sisters and probably St. Joseph too, as a thing to be saved. One of Anna's attractions was that she never tried to change him. She was soft and silent and his own property, and the tenderness with which Mr. Harris looked at her might have been a dagger of suspicion in Mig's heart if it had not been, so conveniently, a needle with which to prick into that vein of blood, which is life, which is power, which is the street, which is money. Mig knew his gods very well.

Mr. Harris and Anna, then, for practical needs; and thin old Father Bailey for occasional sanctuary. Mig's schemes skirted the law. Some day he would be rich and then he could afford to be honest. Meanwhile, he sometimes slipped into Father Bailey's insignificant church whenever he felt the need of divine intervention on a slippery deal. Father Bailey was Episcopalian, whatever that meant, and outside of Mig's usual range of Catholics, Baptists, Pentecostals and God knew what else, but perhaps having better connections. Mig would not touch the Catholics, who ran his family, and the others were too alien, but Father Bailey was, like Richard Harris, a man who could be kept in the pocket.

Today, Mig felt good. He had new shoes, bought without money from a shop window that had been smashed by someone else. His own smashing was delicate and not physical, and it had been directed against the original thief who had made an efficient escape but not an unseen one. Mig had seen him. The shoes, which were slim in the toe and faintly high in the heel, were all that he wanted from the grabbed loot, and they were his in a moment. He was *amigo,* he was Miguel, he would not tell anyone what he had seen, and the shoes were beautiful. Sometimes he was almost disgusted that things were so easy.

But not today. Today he shone in the sun and dazzled the girls who turned to gaze after him. He felt too rich to need Mr. Harris, too secure to need Father Bailey. He even directed a bland wink toward a policeman, an untrustworthy man who had a reputation for not being hungry and therefore must be assumed, in Mig's eyes, to have made his pile already. Mig did not call policemen pigs, or, more currently, fugs; he called them "officer" or "sir" to their faces and "mister" when he talked about them. This device was like carrying a small silver penknife; no one could tell exactly what it intended. The polite words could be adjusted by the tone of his voice, and tone is not quite cause for trouble. And the word *mister* to his friends—who were not very clever—could mean intimacy or contempt or even pass, two-syllabled, as a gutter word.

He did not know all this about his own methods but he felt it, and he certainly recognized that his gentility was useful. It gave him a gloss. The wave of the cop's hand in acknowledgment now might reflect surprise or indifference or a swat at a fly, but for the outsider, for that eternal audience to which Mig played, it was recognition. When he had that and money too, he often thought, he would not even mind going back to school and learning to write and talk and read like Richard Harris, who had a college degree but who was not really clever, only very easy to use. (He planned to go back to school the way he sometimes planned to be a great television star. He had only to dream of it, and it would come about without effort, like the shoes.)

Now, he bought, out of his sudden generosity and wealth, a candy bar for Anna. He never gave her money except to buy their food, but sometimes he gave her things. He avoided asking her what she would like to have, because one of the few whole sentences she had ever said to him was about a doll she had left behind at home. She missed it, she said softly. He would not buy her another one, though he did not quite know why, only that the idea frightened him, and he had a fear of fear. What Anna did all day, with no doll to talk to while he prowled the streets, he did not know either. Once he had brought her a women's magazine, picked out of a trash can, limp and sticky with spilled beer, and she still had it and worked on some of the words but kept it for love of the colored pictures. On the day he knew himself to be rich, he would get her a maple bedroom set from the window of Seeder's Furniture Store. Unless, by that day, he had found the girl who existed just beyond his present reach, blonde as Anna was dark, eager as Anna was timid, American as Anna was still Italian in spite of the melting generations behind her. The girl would be obliging. Anna was not obliging, she was mute.

Mig's dreamed blonde would cry out in ecstasy, or he hoped she would. He was not, in all honesty, certain of the extent of his powers, and it had to be admitted that his first experience had been tentative and confused, although by the time he had come to Anna, his self-esteem was considerable and she could not damage it. But he could not stay with Anna forever, and the day of his dream would come, not in color TV but in the flesh. Again, like the shoes.

He took the candy bar out of his pocket, peeled back the wrapping and took a neat edgewise bite. Then he refolded the paper and returned the gift to his pocket, his mark upon it and his young juices faintly appeased by sugar. She would be just as pleased to have what was left by him as to have it whole. She served him very well, and she was no problem. Or so he thought.

3

I should remember never to go back and read what I have written the day before.

Having done so, I am now caught in a lie, which I am reluctant to confess because it is a well-expressed one. (Aphorism for the day: Fiction is a Well-expressed Lie.) What I said about Jeannie leaves, to put it graciously, an incomplete impression. Jeannie was a nice girl and very kind to me, and she was certainly high-hearted, thick-legged and with revolutionary tendencies, but she never shared my sheets. I had interesting moments of enthusiasm, inconveniently accompanied by a loss of nerve, and, by the time that I found she had a reputation for falling backwards, I had also—again inconveniently—learned to distrust the smug heroes who gave her that reputation. Down with thought!

Somewhere—in some absent notebook full of clever collector's phrases and memos for Mrs. Detty who is a social worker (*her* legs are thin, good God, poor soul! she runs them off trying to make poverty workable) —somewhere, I have Jeannie's telephone number. She gave it to me when she left the Foundation's employment, very casually, and went to live in the West 30's with a girl named Arlene who works in a publishing house. Jeannie, in one last loyal throe, offered to offer my novel to Arlene, and I can clearly remember my outrage at being invited to go in so, by the back door with my hat in my hand.

My real revenge, I can see now, has not been giving Jeannie a complaisant reputation, but giving her thick legs. They were not thick, but sturdy, and most hopefully observed. Perhaps I should try to find that telephone number. Perhaps I should swallow my pride and ask her to give my novel to Arlene, Arlene who works in a publishing house and no doubt serves her boss well in more ways than one.

Let that stand. But, in reality, Arlene is surely nothing more than a nice, plain, dutiful girl who types up the biographies of best-selling authors and thrills to their sublimated nearness. Or a fat jolly girl in tight shoes? I can make a hundred wax dolls out of Arlene and stick pins into all of them—Creative Writing is what we call this interesting process. Poor Arlene, she is only Jeannie's friend, and it was Jeannie who wounded my green young spirit.

I am full of bile tonight, choked with it. And I had better admit the reason, which might be therapeutic in cold print.

Mig was here, less than an hour ago. He came dancing impatiently at the street door, and I went down two flights of stairs to let him in. I should have heard what he had to say on the doorstep and then turned him away, as I have always done before, but this time I broke my rule and let him come up here and talk. My only rule! Never let any of them commit trespass. Work with them *out there,* the Foundation told me. Mrs. Detty said, "Try to cut them off at the end of the day, forget them, go to the movies." "Run like hell," a young intern advised, patiently unsnarling me from the devoted clutch of a walking skeleton with greasy, carefully combed hair. "Run like hell, they stick to you like dirty cobwebs."

I think I let Mig in because of his shoes. They were new ones, and he was proud of them and proud of having earned the money himself, helping out as a stacker in a print shop on a rush job. God-awful fake alligator shoes, but I was pleased with them because they represent a small victory for me. I pushed my luck and asked him if he had bought anything for Anna out of his money, and he shrugged and said no. What I should have done then was to say good-night, but I had one triumph sweet on my tongue and I thought I could create another. Also it was cold and damp on the doorstep, and my land-lady, who is a sort of clean-shaven female and of whom I am honestly afraid, was yelling at us from one of her owl-holes which she lines with straw and dead mice.

Still, I could certainly have told Mig to go home. I did not.

He was interested in my room; looked around as if he owned it; picked up the bronze paperweight that I bought at a flea market, which is only painted-bronze and ugly as sin now that I know it is not antique; shook an opened beer can to see if it was empty; made himself at home like a thin cat in out of the cold. He *is* too thin, eyes like pools. Mrs. Detty loves him and would draw him to her bosom if she had one. I am not sure that I even like him, but he is very important to me. What do I want to do with him? Write a report, perhaps? Case D: meager, neurotic tomcat, snatched from the burning, saved for society, turned into a MAN.

I started in on him about Anna. I had seen her that morning, slowly pushing nickels and dimes across a butcher's counter, and I thought that Mig would eat but I was not sure that she would. Mig was born scrawny, probably wailed up at his mother with cheeks already sunk over gumless baby jaws, blue under his eyes like so many of them, his hands jerking, not fat-baby hands but little twigs. And, for all that, quite tough. He'll outlive everybody. It's Anna who is not eating, her soft brown eyes getting too big for her round face. She is a lost kitten to his tom, and I think she is sick. Mig says she is never sick. He says he bought her a candy bar, come to think of it, and she ate all of it and a pizza too. I agree with him that she must have a good stomach, but I tell him sternly that, if he can buy fancy shoes for himself, he can buy something better than pizza and a candy bar for Anna.

He, therefore, stopped listening, and I had to spend the next fifteen minutes using advanced psychology to loosen up his goddam ears. When I offered him a beer, he asked for a coke instead. He has a hollow sweet tooth, and I suppose his gift of the candy bar was really a gift. If he loves anybody, he probably loves Anna, and just before he left he suddenly announced that he was going to buy her a cross on a gold chain. Big of him! He is planning to have it blessed by Father Bailey, and I did not point out that he is mixing his religions, since Anna must be Catholic to her bones and Father Bailey is Episcopalian. I don't know how the good man will respond to the problem of blessing a Catholic cross for a Catholic neck. Nor do I much care.

I'm resolutely anti-clerical. It's my only creed.

4

He came in off the street early, around midnight, very well pleased with having at last made his way into Mr. Harris's room. He had not thought highly of it, the chairs were shabby, the couch sagged, the paint was peeling, and it was all a disappointment because, certainly, anyone working for a Foundation must be rich. It would be useful to know just where Mr. Harris kept his cash, not to steal it because that would be dangerous as well as ungrateful, but just as a piece of the kind of information that Mig liked to possess.

His own room was dark as he came into it, and out of the dark Anna's voice said his name as it always did, irritating him by its dependence but at the same time making him feel powerful because she had no real existence, alone here, until he came. He thought vaguely that he might give her a picture of himself in a gilt heart to hang around her neck, instead of the cross which was going to be a nuisance, especially if he really meant to have it blessed. The cross had attracted him just as long as he was telling about it, and it had already begun to melt into nothing in his mind. The gilt heart would follow it. The idea bored him, as so many things did, and he did not really care to give her anything.

He said sharply, "Why can't you turn on the light?" and he heard her murmur. He went in the blindfold-dark to the middle of the room and groped for the string of the light pull. It was a feeble bulb, high up against a dirty ceiling, and it stained the room more than it lit it. Anna was sitting on the bed, wrapped in a gray blanket, the same old magazine he had given her open on her knees as if she could read it there in the dark of the room and the dark of her illiteracy. She looked wan, colorless, and his heart gave an angry knock of protest against his ribs before he could tell himself that it was the bad light.

If she was sick, he would have to get rid of her somehow. He did not want to get rid of her; therefore, she was not sick.

He told her she was stupid and she nodded such piteous agreement, looking up at him with soft eyes, that he felt a surge of real fury and snatched the magazine away and threw it across the room. He would have thrown it out of the window, but the window was closed. She gave a little mewing cry.

He said a gutter obscenity. He had a few, and they were shared by every three-year-old and every junkie on the street so they had no magic and little value, but he used them against Anna because he knew she shrank from them. He had never struck her, he never intended to. Something warned him that he would not know what to do afterwards.

He said "Who came?" and she said "I was out" and he nodded. The room cost him nothing, only an easy arrangement with the man whose name he did not wish to know. Two hours a day it belonged to that man, and who met with who during those two hours was nothing to Mig. Anna had come back early once and had been sworn at, she said, and she had said something too about some very small packages. Mig had told her that he didn't want to know anything about it. Officially, the room had been given to him for his young-man charm, and if any cop should ever ask him about it, he had only to mutter and look ashamed, and the cop would give a snort of disgust and let it go at that. He, Mig, would be perfectly clean.

. He sat down on the bed and took off his beautiful shoes and smiled at them. Then he said, "Anna, come here, Anna," and she came like the little leashed dog that she was, and he quite unexpectedly pulled her down beside him and cradled her against his chest. She flowed against him, there was no other word for it, in absolute trust. He leaned his head back against the wall and closed his eyes, pretending to himself that she was the girl that he was going to have and take some day, whose taking would be very sweet and who would make him a man . . . . .

His conceit flared. He was a man already and he sat up, prepared to prove it on Anna, and then, because it was after midnight and he had the new shoes and the day had been so successful, he was overtaken by a sort of fat content. "Anna, Anna," he said. "Anna, Anna-Anna."

She lifted her face. She did not look sick at all. The light was bad, and she looked almost beautiful. Some men might envy him. Many more would envy him when he was rich, and some day he would be rich and everything of which he now despaired would become possible. He would find a way to be rich, very soon. He thought of what happened here, in this room, in the two hours that he and Anna stayed away from it, and he knew perfectly well what happened and he knew that he could not touch it. In jail, it was impossible to grow rich.

But it might be useful to know more about what went on in those two hours. There were ways of getting beautiful shoes without breaking store windows. There were ways of finding out useful things and of risking other necks, and he was very good at such ways.

Sitting there on the bed, he became in that moment of dream incredibly rich. He did not walk the street, he owned it, and his American girl owned it with him and she walked at his side with her long legs and her long yellow hair. He laughed out loud in pure luxury, sat up abruptly and said, "I brought you a candy bar." He took it, somewhat damaged, out of his pocket, and saw her sink her teeth into its sweetness as if she would drown herself, and then he yawned and stretched and pushed her away from him, fell back against the hard pillow and slept at once.

He did not even feel the blanket when she covered him up, or herself when she lay down beside him, clutching in her fist, very tightly, the candy-bar wrapper. If he would have let her, she would have smothered him with her love because he let her stay here, but she was a little lost child of Eve and she knew enough not to show too much of how she felt.

She was also very frightened, but she could not tell him about that now, and perhaps if she was very lucky she would never have to tell him at all. She had never in her life been lucky, but tomorrow everything might change because tonight Mig had thought of her and had brought her a candy bar.

She lay against him, saying under her breath, devoutly, "Hail-Mary-full-of-grace" and "Blessed-art-thou-among-women-and-blessed-is-the-fruit-of-thy-womb," and she had absolutely no idea what the prayer meant.

5

Would this interest you, Professor Blount?

I was stopped on the street today by a little black tart, who wanted to know if I could supply her with the name of any place that would teach her how to type. Her own name is Cassy, and she is a pretty little charcoal drawing who shares her boy friend with a thin trick named Irmalee, a cornsilk blonde who is so astonishingly fair that she is almost an albino. Cassy and Irmalee are our school lesson for today, Professor Blount, on Learning How to Live Together. They both wanted the same thing, and I use the word "thing" advisedly—a little sawed-off punk about the size of a pocket jockey with tight pants, waved hair, a slick little grin and the name of Angel. ("They always call them either Angel or Jesus," says Mrs. Detty, as usual inaccurate but just.) Angel, to Cassy and Irmalee, seems to have been the answer to every dream, and there was a six-months vendetta into which razor blades were eventually introduced. Irmalee drew first blood and celebrated it by fainting. Someone called an ambulance, and unconscious Irmalee went to the hospital while bloody Cassy licked her wounded wrist like a cat, and Angel went home, whether to brag or to shudder I do not know.

Theoretically, you have to be dead on this street to rate an ambulance, but by some coincidence Irmalee rated, giving herself such ascendancy that Cassy vowed to carve her up. She went to Irmalee's home (eight people in three rooms) to do it right this time, armed not with a razor but with a switchblade knife. She had a single, pure intention: to make for that pretty white face and to disenchant Angel forever.

Afterwards, Irmalee never talked about it, and no one was able to get the precise truth out of Cassy. All she told Mrs. Detty was that Irmalee cried, she didn't yell, she just cried. Like a baby, said Cassy. But she can't have said it in scorn, because somehow in that miserable dump (vacated by the seven who saw the knife and who were probably not afraid of the knife but were very afraid of being asked later what happened), somehow Irmalee and Cassy joined their silly white-white and black-black hands and agreed to share Angel between them.

I have often wondered how Angel felt, and in fact I have often wondered how they managed it, straightforward girls both of them and, in their way, stimulating. What was marching to tragedy (not big tragedy, we save that for big people) turned into comic opera, and Angel now uses cologne but I don't know whether this is because he is a beneficiary of the girls' generosity or a refugee from a somewhat overwrought sex life. Nobody makes a judgment on them here; they do what they do. Twenty years from now, Angel who went to high school may quite possibly be a bank president, heir to the American Dreaming, while Irmalee and Cassy may have brought forth sons and daughters who will intermarry and produce endless confusion between them down the generations of time. Or be very happy. How the hell would I know?

When I came to these fair streets, O Professor Blount, I made value judgments. I knew every answer, and I might add that I was in a constant state of embarrassment. Now I don't know any answers, and I am never embarrassed, although from time to time I wish that I could be.

Well, perhaps if I re-read my novel now, it would embarrass me. Or perhaps it is, after all, the very good novel that I once knew it was. Me and Jeannie.

However, I was telling Professor Blount a story, a narrative, full of colorful descriptions and sharp characterization. Was I not, dear Professor? You will have noted that I began at the climax, thereby violating the first rule of fiction. I began with the fact that our ignorant little street girl, Cassy, wants to take a course in typing, in order to fit herself for the World Out There. She asks me about it, because I am the one who knows these things, and I stand on a windy corner in this backwash of a world, listening attentively and politely. ("Always be polite," said the Foundation. "It helps them to trust you.") I stand listening to her, and I lift one hand to a cop as he goes by, partly because I know him and partly because I want to impress her. She is not, of course, impressed; she divides cops between "good-lookers" and "not good-lookers," which is what she does with anything male. She also has the typical street problem of recognizing that every cop is not only the enemy of herself but also the enemy of her enemies, which leads to muddled thinking. However, she was pleased by my insouciant wave, a status wave, at this particular specimen who is young, walks tough and, unless he is a moron, is scared for about two-thirds of his working hours. He's right to be scared. It's not a jungle, this street, that would be too easy. It's an antique myth. Its fires light up caves, not houses, and its tigers are saber-toothed. Jungles have boa constrictors; this street has evil spirits.

I wax romantic. This is a simple story, demanding only a simple narrative style. Touching, too! A street girl wants to learn how to type. As I bend my ear and listen gravely, I am informed that Irmalee also wishes to learn to type. I am further informed that they wish to go to a secretarial school, instead of night school, because that will give them class. They have money, Cassy tells me. They have taken back all the money they gave to Angel. (What money? where did it come from? why hasn't he spent it? God, they're crazy.) She tells me how much and I swallow hard and say, yes, they could perhaps take a very *short* course . . . What she hears from me is Yes, yes, they will learn to be expert typists, they will make vast fortunes, they will live in their own apartment with a fur rug, they will marry the son of the boss and move to Westchester.

I mumble something, a mumble which I have perfected. I'll go into the matter, I say. I'll look it up for her. Let me think about it.

Cassy has a real smile. After all these sixteen years of life here, she has a real smile. And she believes me. It's very nice that she believes me. It makes us both feel good.

By next week, I will try to have the name of a good, cheap, efficient and motherly secretarial school. By next week, she and Irmalee will already have forgotten their plans for a brave, new world. Or Angel will have looked at them and said "What money?" Or, which is more likely, the money never really existed at all.

But they will remember that Richard Harris cared, and that he listened. And Richard Harris will never have to say what is so horribly true—that there is very little point in any young girl going to a secretarial school unless she has first learned to read and write at least beyond the fifth-grade reading level.

So why wouldn't a cop be a coward for two-thirds of his day? I am demonstrably a coward for the whole of mine, and, by being a coward, I really make out very well. I shall put Cassy and Irmalee into my report for the Foundation, omitting Angel who can be construed not to be "relevant."

I suppose I ought to get out of this job before I turn into something that I never meant to be. For who am I to call Angel —Cassy and Irmalee's Angel—a "thing"?

6

Mama Kraus had watched the street all morning from her second-floor cave, elbows on the sill and window open to gray weather. She was waiting for the once-a-month arrival of her landlord, whose office address was vague but whose appearance was as prompt as doom.

Mama Kraus believed in obliging him. Twice, she had failed in her duty as tenant, and the second time her landlord had implied nastily that he knew more about her than she might wish him to know and would she prefer the accommodations of a city jail? The first time, her failure to pay had been over-confidence in her ability to swindle. The second time, it had been simple bad management, compounded by a social worker's discovery that Mama Kraus had managed to get herself on Welfare at three different addresses and under two different names—a pleasant arrangement which had given her plenty to live on and to feed the dog as well. Not that she had much feeling for the dog, which was the legacy of a roomer who had shared her bed. (He was a roomer and not a guest, because he had paid for the use of the mattress.) The dog was a bag of bones when it came and was now stout; it kept people away if she told it to, and so she fed it regularly and fed it well. It slept a good deal, but then so did she.

Bored with the memory of her roomer, she turned her mind to the thought of Richard Harris and, if it had been possible for Mama Kraus's face to shape benevolence, it would have done so. The first time she had failed in her rent, Mr. Harris had paid it for her out of money which came from whatever-its-name-was Foundation. She did not believe in the Foundation; she did not for a moment think he was getting money to give away from anything honest or that he was distributing it out of pure good will. She had a number of theories about Richard Harris, and they were all as interesting as they were slanderous.

The payment of the first rent had been something of a coincidence; the second was much more direct. That time, when the landlord came with his greasy out-of-town smile, she had waddled straight to Mr. Harris's room, knocked on his door and instructed him as to her needs. She had counted, rightly, on his being anxious to get rid of her, and he sighed heavily but gave her the money. She tried him only once more, this time not because the rent was due but because money was always useful, and he had said "No" in such a fashion that it was clear he now knew all about her. She had waddled away angrily, telling herself that some day Mr. Harris would have a girl of his own who would need her peculiar kind of help. Reflecting on this now, she sourly revised her prophecy. He was not man enough.

Mama Kraus was called Mama because, over her seedy forty years, she had produced three daughters. Two had gone into some limbo that did not concern her. The third, the youngest, was now in a City institution which had accepted the child who was already nine, under the impression that she belonged to someone else. Nature had played a bitter joke in permitting Mama Kraus to be a mother at all, and Mama, who was as fat as her fat dog and in whose pudding face there burned black eyes as sultry as an odalisque's, would have been the first to agree.

For motherhood, family life, domestic employment (her only job had lasted just one hour) and other graces, Mama Kraus had substituted watching. She watched the street below her window through all the daylight hours and, if she missed anything, it was because she occasionally fell asleep. Her mouth was as tight as her eyes were large, and what she saw she kept to herself.

She had been watching Mig since the day of his arrival. He had a sneaky look at that time, and it was Mama Kraus's experience that sneaky looks often led to interesting revelations. Her theory was that he was mixed up in some kind of organization, and she watched the men who came to his room by day with shrewd, educated attention. In occasional carelessness, these men left the window shade open enough so she could see thin, swift hands and very small packages. She merely studied them, said nothing, only observed in her small pleased mind that Mig would be in trouble some day. She did not know how neatly he had foreseen that trouble and how, already, he was prepared to talk his way out of it.

Mama Kraus did not really care about Mig, or what happened to Mig or even who might kill Mig, until Anna came to live in the room with him. She did not like Anna at all, for a subterranean dark reason she could never have recognized. Anna was too much like that silent nine-year-old child, ward of the City, officially born to some other mother, who had—to her real mother's knowledge—cried only once and then in absolute silence.

Somewhere under all that flesh and beyond the sultry black eyes, Mama Kraus had once possessed a heart, but it had not shriveled as small hearts so often do. It had decayed. Having chosen not to like Anna, she soon found it pleasantly easy to wish her ill and to treat her, perversely, with an attentiveness, a concern, that looked very like affection.

Mig, who had observed this, supposed that it was directed at himself. He was usefully attractive to women of all ages, but he made no use of Mama Kraus because he had no need of her. She was only a blob of black-eyed fat crouched at a window, staring at the street. When she told him that his girl looked sick, his indifference changed to the hatred he felt for anyone who gave him warnings, since he believed that warnings cause disaster rather than prophesy it. He said curtly that Anna was coming down with a virus, a word he had heard somewhere. Then he turned on his heel and went back to his room to face Anna with the wretched and inexcusable fact of her advertised mortality and to demand that she deny it.

He found her—as so often lately—curled on the bed with a coat over her legs and her face buried in the pillow. Her long dark hair needed washing, and it was pulled back tight and bound with a piece of string. She looked to Mig suddenly unappetizing. Mama's warning was curdling inside him already, and for just a minute if he had had any place in the world to run to, he would have run there.

She woke instantly at the sound of the door but lay without moving, her eyes still closed in that peculiar world she had known for so long now, where darkness of any kind was more friendly than light. She knew exactly how he looked standing in the middle of the room, and she knew he was very beautiful and that she loved him, and her heart tore.

"Anna? You sick?"

She turned her head back into the daylight world, pushed the coat off her feet and struggled up, giving him the sweet, timid, disastrous smile that was like a hand raised to ward off a blow. (If she ever saw her mother again—and, of course, she would not—that was the one thing she would be able to say. Mig had never struck her.) She shook her head in violent denial of his question, and to prove how very well and strong she was she jumped to her feet and was quick and clumsy where usually she was quick and neat.

He saw that. He also saw that the skin under her eyes was stretched very tight and the shadows were more purple than blue. In the free world of no responsibilities, there is, for the world's Migs, one fear that always lies close to the surface. Now, before he could ward it off, it had pounced on him and he heard himself say, "Anna. You going to have a kid?"

In that ten seconds while he waited for her answer, he knew if she said yes, he would have to throw her out. . . . Someone else's kid! Go home to your mother! . . . He had a feeling that was neither remorse nor anger but something else, and it stupefied him because he knew that she meant nothing to him and never had. Only a considerable convenience in the arrangements of a life that was becoming increasingly well arranged.

"Anna?"

The smile she gave him was not the one he was used to. It was, astonishingly, the kind of smile that his dreamed American blonde might have given, bright, confident, almost gay. She said "Oh no, Mig!" and she almost sounded as if she might be laughing at him.

His relief was intense, although he told himself that, if Anna had been in trouble, it would have been her own fault. (He supposed. She could look after herself. Her mother would have told her about things. She was not a child.) He was delighted, and the delight went to his head. He would spit in Mama Kraus's face, she was an old whore anyway and no good to anyone.

He strode to Anna, all man again, and pulled her against him and kissed her exactly as he would have kissed his blonde girl, only he knew that this was Anna and he kissed her that way anyhow.

She felt hope, as sudden and wild as his seizing. Perhaps this was the day when everything would change, and everything would be good in a new and shining creation. She knew so little, she could be wrong about all the sickness and the warnings?

And, if she was not wrong, there were still things that could be done. Mig need never know anything at all, nothing, ever. She clung to him, tightly, like a child.

7

We appear to have a nice little racket operating in these parts, which has earned the attention of the police. A cop has just come to call. I am honored. He is honored. He represents Law and Order, and I represent Philanthropy, words which we avoid as they have lately fallen into disrepute. But, because he came to my room and displayed his detective's shield cupped in his hand and because I offered him coffee (the Foundation wouldn't have approved anything more potent, and I don't know how his captain would feel about it—indifferent, perhaps?) and showed him some notes I was making for my current report, we were able to be Law & Order & Philanthropy together like a respectable corporate body.

I found myself remembering the first time I ever sat down to talk to a cop as man to man. It was a thrilling experience, I do assure you, sir. That cop deferred to me and I felt twelve feet high, not realizing that he was not talking to me but to the Foundation. He was just past being a rookie, fresh and eager from the Academy, and in my way I was a rookie too so we had a bond. We both felt very essential to civilization, and we spoke in quick, soft monosyllables. I talked like a world banker, and he talked like the FBI, and we enjoyed ourselves enormously. I don't remember now why he came; probably someone had stolen the top of a garbage can. Something monumental. (What do they use the tops of garbage cans for? The kids use them as shields in vicious street fighting, I know that, clanking like Crusaders, but there must be some other use that is more profitable. Somewhere there has to be a pawnbroker who deals exclusively in the tops of garbage cans. God rest his soul.)

But now, even in the brotherhood of Law and Order, with a detective sitting in my best chair (better chair, I should say pedantically; I only own two), I no longer feel twelve feet tall, and I miss the sensation. When I started this job, I always felt that way. I could work eighteen hours, eat and drink anything, see and hear any filth, make a hundred mistakes a day, make a fool of myself at every corner, and still feel as if I was——

"Clothed with the heavens and crowned with the stars."

That's from Thomas Traherne, English Lit., I didn't realize I would still remember it. One of the books I brought up here with me is his Centuries of Meditation, but I've never opened it from that day to this. First, I was too excited to read Great Literature and anyway, so high was my self-esteem, I knew everything it had to tell me. And now I avoid it because it says too much and says it too well and I feel excluded. Even on the radio, when I get Beethoven, I switch to rock and roll. Not because I like it much, but because Beethoven demands attention and I don't want to attend. Not while I can sit here and chirp to my typewriter these little nuggets of philosophy and character sketches drawn straight from life. The Real Thing—just like a TV commercial.

Five-finger exercises.

Back to Law and Order, sitting in my chair, drinking my coffee. He was a pleasant guy named Sloan, heavy, deliberate. I wouldn't want him on my tail. The small gang that he came to talk to me about evidently consists of two or three youths (he thinks) who are engaged in blackmailing another group of about ten youths (he believes) who are responsible for a continuous and effective series of fast-grab robberies through smashed windows, off fire escapes, down shafts. Watch your typewriter, he says. It's a junk heap, I tell him, and he looks at it appraisingly, and then at me. Lie number one, he says to himself; wants to be one of the boys, a street urchin right out of a bank window.

"The top kids work on a percentage of the take, apparently," he goes on, and I answer nastily and without thinking, "What New York's Finest would call a cut."

He put his coffee cup down on the table, and then he lit a cigarette and just looked at me. I felt small. He had come in doing his job, and it was my job to do mine, not to make wisecracks that were straight out of kindergarten. (And even now I can write that and admire myself for being so perceptive about my own stupidities. Hell, what I need is someone who will be kind to me!)

I wanted to apologize and heard myself stammering, so I got up and went over to the hot plate for the coffee pot. He said, to my back, "Tell you something, Mr. Harris. There's plenty of hungry cops around, and some of them get found out. And, when they're found out, some of them get busted. But I've got a wife and three kids and I'm not prepared to risk my job for a handful of hay." He sighed. "Can we talk now?"

I said I was sorry, without being fancy about it, and the smell of sulphur went out of the room. He gave a curt nod and went on talking to me about his young masterminds, wanting to know if I'd heard any street telegrams. They operate, he said, like an illegal shoo-fly squad, watching the stealing, noting the stealers, and then stepping in for their—cut, he said. (He needn't have said it; I'd already got the message.)

I repeated that it was all news to me, and even while I was saying it, I heard a door shut tight inside my head. He had described the top group as being cool, quick, sure of itself; he said whoever was king was a very smart kid and very careful.

He waited to see if I was going to say anything, and when I didn't, he shrugged and went on. "Naturally, we'd like to know a bit more."

I asked him, cautiously, if it was the kind of crime they could make a court case of, and he laughed and used a word that I suppose was obscene but was new to me and unspellable. "It's not indictable," he added, "if that's what you mean. We can't pin anything down at the moment. No, they could be useful to us, that's all. They know where some of the action is, and if we knew who the watchers were, maybe we could tie up the little gentlemen they're watching."

"Little gentlemen" sounded explicit and nasty; I thought I might not care to be a little gentleman. I said I would keep my eyes open, and thank you, officer. "That's what you want from me, isn't it?" said the Foundation, speaking in my voice, very brisk and businesslike.

He didn't say anything for a minute or two, and then he said "Yeah" and got to his feet. He held out his hand. I took it. Two strong men came face to face in the best Kipling style, and I was the first to look down at the table, just to see if the coffee pot was keeping well.

I said "Yeah" too. It sounded like a great piece of dialogue.

I saw him to the door like a butler, and, standing in the doorway, he said "Skipper says you're doing a good job." He then left me, not troubling to find out if I knew that Skipper means precinct captain or to measure the gratitude and relief that clutched my flattered heart.

Only now, reading back over what I have written, I can see that my detective friend is a very shrewd character, and that Mig—if Mig is the leader, as he obviously suspects—had better walk carefully. I could warn him, but why should I? If he is only to be the tied goat to catch the tiger, let him be that.

I could talk to Father Bailey about him, I suppose. I've never wanted to, for my own good and bad reasons, but Mig is getting too much for me in some ways. Maybe Father Bailey would know about Anna. Maybe she really is sick.

But what it comes down to is that I don't want advice from a churchman. Neither Father Bailey nor Thomas Traherne. Nor, thank you, even from God.

8

Mig waited on the street corner until the detective had gone, and then he decided not to visit Mr. Harris tonight at all. He knew that the visitor was Police, not because you can tell a fug by his walk (a folk tale) but because a thin little piece of blue cheese named Ernie had pointed him out. Ernie had a gift for picking up scraps of information, which he carried to Mig like an alley cat carrying a fishhead. Some of the fishheads were no good, but ever so often there would be one worth chewing on.

There could be any number of reasons why Mr. Harris was having this particular visitor, but, when you are running, it is natural to believe that anyone going in the same direction is chasing you. Not that Mig was running, or intended to, but the hare is not the only animal in the forest that keeps its ears high and its nerves stretched tight. Some day Mig planned to be a big enough animal not to care. When that day came, *they* would listen for *his* footsteps, not the other way around as it was now.

He walked back home, thinking neatly and rapidly and whistling between his teeth. The trouble was that Ernie, who had been working obediently as hired help, now wanted to join the bosses, and Mig was going to have to accept him, partly because he already knew so much and partly because he could slide like an eel through the city's soft currents. At the moment, Ernie was working both sides of the street; he was picking the places to loot (which was boss work) and then he was moving in personally, and jauntily, with the looters. For all that he looked like a stepped-on cockroach, he was unbelievably good at this part of the program, carrying away twice as much as anyone else and as fast as a cat's tail.

Mig knew also, with indifference, that Ernie idolized him, and he had already made use of this vulnerable condition by indicating that, on the next grab, a portable TV set would be very acceptable tribute. Ernie vowed prompt delivery like any department store, and Mig took satisfaction in picturing himself bringing the set home to Anna. He also pictured himself telling her flatly that she must not touch it, since she was clumsy and had once broken a pocket radio. The idea of having a TV set pleased him. It would fill in some of the empty-handed boredom that plagued his days, only because the things that other people had—things like TV sets—were not available to him. Later, he would have all these things, and many more.

He stopped thinking about his endless, unfilled desires long enough to make an obscene proposal to a passing, long-haired, high-gaited bella (he wouldn't have known how to carry it out if she had been agreeable), and she looked straight through him and clean out the other side. He shrugged, more relieved than wounded, although he had hoped to impress and most girls would at least have sniggered. He dismissed her as a rag, returned to his thought of Ernie and resolved to keep him in line and never let him know how useful he was. For a moment, Mig saw himself as a black spider, sitting in a web of communication posts, issuing orders—a television dream in living color with the inevitable blonde in the center of it. Some day the tight skirt and the long, hard look would be sorry for what she had missed.

He pulled his mind off her and back to Ernie, felt for the cigarettes he carried loose in his pocket, broke one clumsily, swore and lit another. He carried them loose in his pocket to make them look like the real sticks, but the truth was that the only time he had smoked grass it had made him sick, mean and dazed. He hinted exotic things about his own supply of cigarettes, but, if anyone insisted on smoking one of them, he just laughed in the fallen face, so that Up-Johnny was the fool, not him. He was clean too, in case (God forbid) he was ever picked up, and that suited him perfectly.

That was going to be one of the troubles about Ernie. If Ernie got caught by the cops at the low end, he might just sing at the high one, which was what Mig wanted least. For his own part, he was not doing anything provably illegal; if the Ernies chose to hand over objects they picked up around town, it was none of Mig's business where the objects came from. Even if Ernie did talk, to some cop, in some stationhouse room, Mig would still be clean.

Tomorrow night was already set up, and it was too late to make any changes, except perhaps to drop in on Father Bailey's insignificant storefront church with the cross over the doorway. Mig had performed this rite from time to time, ever since the day he had possessed, in all the world, exactly one five-dollar bill and had recklessly handed it over to a bookie in the Bronx. The Bronx, for Godssake! He couldn't even remember what he had been doing in the Bronx.

The five dollars had been placed on the nose of a long-shot named Ego, which the bookie told him meant Eye. After he had placed his crazy bet, Mig had walked the streets muttering and swearing, and, when he found the cross-signed, window-on-the-street church in front of him, it seemed as if it had moved to block his path. He slipped inside mindlessly, nothing to lose and perhaps something to gain, and, kneeling there in its weekday, unlocked shelter, he had prayed for Ego to come in first, requesting nothing less than a miracle.

Ego won by a length, and from that day on Mig had a cautious belief in the power of Father Bailey's church to stave off calamity. He used this power infrequently, and only for important things, but tomorrow was important. Head around the door ought to be enough; he need not kneel. Mig saw no reason why God would want to put him at a disadvantage, and daylight was still abroad.

I went to see Father Bailey in order to glean such information as he might have about Mig. My gleaning was not rewarded.

I have never really talked to the good man before, not in the three years I have been here. Street chats, yes. Corner conferences. How is Mrs. Jackson's baby: buried yesterday? back at school? grown up and gone to jail? hung up on heroin? the Ways of the Lord are strange indeed. I know Father Bailey's answers before he makes them, as I know his clerical collar (threadbare), his hat (battered and clinging to his head by, I suppose, friction) and the way he elbows through the streets, thrusting himself forward, his old nose eager and his old eyes a shortsighted fading blue.

Long before I came, his church burned down. No one ever rebuilt it, but he stayed on, and his congregation (of two, of six, of nobody) gathers now in his storefront-cathedral and, whatever the Church Fathers may have thought of him once, they ignore him now. Maybe they don't even know that he's up here. Maybe they lost him somewhere in the ecclesiastical records, a true clerical error. Or at Epiphany, even now, is he remembered in prayer by some trembling old verger, mumbling "our dear Father Bailey"? Has he been transubstantiated, rising like a phoenix from the ashes of his church? The street story is that the small, well-made church went up in a single flame. It is also an authenticated fact that the Cross on its brick front was never found, or that the Cross was found and is the one now over the storefront, or that the Cross was found by looters and melted down, or that there never was a Cross at all.

I believe the transubstantiation theory, which would account for the fact that he is a difficult man to find at whatever hour one looks for him. (Or have I confused transubstantiation with deliquescence?) Sometimes he can be traced through the black woman who works for him, a small fierce creature so determinedly Afro that she looks like a puppet bushman. She has a high sweet voice that hums in the ear, and it is understood that she "does" his church for him. I do not know what she "does," creeping about, spitting on her dirty cloth to polish the makeshift altar rail, but I do know that he treats her with uncommon respect, and this may be why she works for him. Respect for human beings is not that common around here . . . . .

Well, well. There was certainly a time when I would have been shocked to find myself writing that. I thought once that respect for humanity was what it was all about, and that, up here, among the "real" people, I would find it. I suppose that could be called naive. A dirty-mouthed and drunk member of the Establishment, sprawled and spewing at a country-club bar, is no different from a dirty-mouthed and drunk member of the Submerged, sprawled and spewing in a gutter, and both are bums. And yet I still say "my brother" more easily about the penniless than about the moneyed. O stout Foundation Fraternity, did you hire an inverted snob? Sure you did. An inverted snob was what you wanted, and I am a good-hearted one and very obedient and you pay me adequately. Certainly I am not the first man to stare into a dark corner and ask Why? but, naturally, you prefer that I do so on my own time.

Professor Blount would tell me to avoid these endless

philosophical insertions, but Professor Blount is not here and I am. Professor Blount would also tell me that my narrative style is undisciplined.

So be it. I looked for Father Bailey in a rather aimless way, almost domestically like a housewife shaking out rugs and looking for beetles. Several people could probably have told me where to find the old man, but I didn't want to ask because talk raves up and down these streets like an Irish village—"And what would Misther Harris be wantin' wi' Father Bailey the day?" I even received a tirra-lirra-Killarney-type blessing from a sick, bleary lath of a man who is conditioned to curse me on sight and who, this time, chose to croon. He was either in an alcoholic heaven (he never shoots any stuff; he says that drugs are unclean, drawing his voice aside like the skirts of a Victorian lady in a piggery), or else the day's sunshine had worked itself into his draggy bones and he saw me as a fuzzy and pleasing object with gold edges. I would like to believe it was the sunshine because I am romantic by nature, put me down in Ireland and I would wed dark Rosaleen. (Regret it too, probably.) And you are absolutely correct, Professor Blount, about my narrative style. But do I not play nicely upon the harp? And who knows? The day may yet come when I will be seized once more by the wholesome desire to write another novel and there will be another Jeannie and I will walk in the garden of Manhattan again and admire all the simple beauties of life, like crocuses and Tiffany's and the shapes of girls.

I'm doing all this on just one beer. Give me back, oh, give me back my narrative technique, I am floundering, I am lost. "I looked for Father Bailey. I found Father Bailey." Go on from there. Rewrite this in second draft, explain to the editorial department about battle fatigue, *they'll* understand. Right on, man.

Father Bailey was at home, where I finally went to find him. He has two rooms to my one, and he has somehow managed to get ten times the stuff into them. I used to picture him living an ascetic life, narrow cot, wafers and water, one modest light bulb. On the contrary, the place is a thrift shop of clutter; bits of china; ballpoint pens in six colors; paper cups; boxes and boxes of Kleenex; two alarm clocks, back to back; balls of string; even a birdcage without a bird. Books, of course, those I understand about, but why three editions of Sumpter & Hoyle's *Analysis of Credibilities?* Is he a kleptomaniac?

He was surprised to find me on his third-floor landing (he lives, appropriately, one flight nearer Heaven than I do), and, when he stood aside to let me pass, I thought I caught the word "housecleaning." He had a bathrobe on and I do not believe he was doing anything constructive at all, but I felt guilty for disturbing him and offered to leave. He said no, no (he is a man who says no, no and yes, yes a great deal) and he took a cushion off a chair and put it on the table and then put it back on the chair again since it was one of the few things in the room which had been in the right place from the start. Something about his very real and anxious hospitality made me feel suddenly awkward and all of sixteen years old. I towered with disgusting healthiness over his frailty and knew that I ought to have wiped my four great paws on the doormat and stayed outside.

I sat down, and he offered me coffee, or beer, or tea. I chose tea because I thought it would cause him less trouble. It caused him no trouble at all, he simply asked me to make my own. I did this meekly, finding the implements and only forgetting that the water should be poured on the teabag rather than the teabag swished around in the water. However, it turned out drinkable, and I had time while the water was boiling to stare at the uncluttered wall (uncluttered? how had it escaped him?) and wonder how to introduce the subject of Mig.

I produced two cups of acceptable tea, flanked by pink

plastic spoons, and bore them back to him with some pride. He cleared a place on the table with one hand and accepted his teacup with the other. I took a chair, sat on the edge of it and sipped my brew, meditating on how we must look—two gentlemen of the old school having their cuppa while the bombs of riot/poverty/sorrow/hell thunder down on the pavement outside.

I meditated in hot-tongued silence, and he stirred. After a while, he withdrew his plastic spoon which appeared to have melted slightly, gazed at it and put it on the table inside one of the boxes of Kleenex. He then said, "I wonder if you know a man named Rafe Pollo."

I said, "Yes. He's mad. Always was."

He raised his eyes from his teacup. "You've been here—how long?" His voice was conspicuously gentle, which annoyed me. I said stiffly, "Almost three years," perfectly aware that Father Bailey had been in these parts many years longer and that Pollo, with his name that sounded like some gigantic green parrot, had once been perfectly sane.

He nodded absently and started to hunt out that pink plastic spoon from the box he had put it in. I said with what I trust was veiled irritation, "What about Pollo?"

"He's been committed. This morning."

I said instantly, off the top of my head, not thinking, "Oh God no!" It was a stupid reaction because Pollo was certain to end behind walls of one kind or another, and this was all for the best, of course. But he was so harmless, a crazy old horse in a wild meadow and, in his way, he was free, there was sky around him. I felt unexpectedly sick, and I said lamely, "I don't see why. He left everybody alone. They left him alone." Tom Fool, I thought. Poor Tom's a-cold.

Father Bailey put his cup down on the table and looked at me sympathetically, which I did not think it was his place to do, but I asked "Why?" again because I wanted to know. I am a card file of human events.

"It seems he has a daughter," Father Bailey said, "who certified him. I don't know who told her to do it."

"Banishment," I said, still thinking of Lear and feeling depressed out of all reason. Pollo would be dead in two years anyway, his brain was maggoty, maybe it was better to put him away safe.

We sat there, trying to worry our way through a sadness that was not really ours. After a while I shook myself out of it (not wanting to think of the times I might have gone to see Pollo, only it could always wait till tomorrow) and I said, somewhat defensively I suppose, "Well, I don't know what I can do about it." As he didn't answer, I dropped the subject and changed to the one I had come about. "Did you get paid a visit by Detective Sloan?"

He nodded. "About Mig."

I waited. He waited. He was relaxed and I was not, so I was the first to speak. I said, "He doesn't seem to think the kid's in trouble really, he didn't even mention his name, you know. Just that they were watching. I didn't know what to say to him, I thought you might have noticed something . . ." The technique of not answering is always very productive with me. I start to talk more than I intend to and, the moment I realize it, I shut up too fast. I shut up.

Father Bailey had found his pink plastic spoon. He sighed, put it into the saucer and said, "Mrs. Larson tells me she saw Mig at the back of our church last night. Slipped in and out, she said."

It sounded like a ballad, a-slippin' in and out among the grasses-o. "Mrs. Larson?"

"She cleans for me."

"The little bushy one with the black face? She's named *Larson?*" I was sorry the minute I said it, convicting myself of that automatic cliché, the law of black/white names, black/white faces, black/white jobs. For all I knew, Mrs. Larson might be the wife of some good Swedish seafarer, hearty and blue-eyed and bearded. (Or a Swedish bootblack? Talk about clichés! I have a well-worn highway in my brain where all my stereotypes travel; it runs on a parallel line with that highway where I smugly see all men as brothers.) "All right," I said, politely because he had left me time to work it out. "So she's Mrs. Larson."

He said soberly, "I'm not sure that she's entitled to the Mrs., but she prefers it."

I switched subjects. "Does it mean anything?"

"Mig's coming to church? Well, yes, I'm afraid that it does. In fact, I've been wondering if I ought to mention it to Detective Sloan."

I said frankly that I didn't know what he was talking about, and he apologized and said no, no, of course I didn't. "But it's my impression," he went on, "that Mig appears in my church only when he's planning something. Unless I misunderstand him, he feels a vague need for protection and brings a prayer to my church to be—" He paused. "Registered."

"Why *your* church?"

He made a gesture with his cup and saucer and that fun-loving plastic spoon of his fell on the floor. I got down on my knees to retrieve it, and he said to the top of my listening head, "It's pure superstition with him, Mr. Harris."

I rose from the floor, handed him his spoon and said heartily, "Maybe he likes you."

"Well, yes, he may. But he would like me even better if I had a jewel in my forehead.—Thank you very much, I'm short of spoons. More tea?" I declined, and he then said that he didn't suppose I would really feel that his church was a church at all.

I wanted to console him for his sad little church that was not a church at all, and at the same time I didn't want him to get any idea that I would take off my hat and bow three times to the East at the mere mention of the holy place, and the result was that I achieved no response at all. Anyway, I think now, looking back, that I was resentful about his having been so shrewd about Mig. I asked him if he had seen Anna lately.

"Yesterday. She doesn't look well."

"She never does." I thought of how she had looked the last time I saw her, her face peaked and her eyes enormous, like a kitten needing only to be stroked so it could die purring. "She'll die, you know," I said angrily, "she'll die on his hands."

He looked up at me. "Why do you think so?"

"Because that's the way things are in this God-damned oasis in hell." I didn't say goddam, I said God-damned, very clearly. The accreditation and the complacency of Father Bailey's calling made me suddenly angry. I felt like hitting somebody, and I said with deliberate rudeness, "Hope is your trade, not mine."

"It's wrong?" he said.

I regretted having come. The last thing I had been looking for was a theological argument on the relative merits of hope and despair, heaven and hell. I suppose I sounded sullen. "It's just a little—" What I wanted to say was that I found him just too smoothly aristocratic, among all us little peasants, but it sounded shanty. "It's just a little—"

"Insensitive?"

Yes, that was what I meant, one adequate word nicely summing up my rather fancy analogy. I don't know whether I resented his perception or his word-selection more. I said, "Well? Isn't it?"

He didn't answer for such a long time that I felt my feet growing to the rug and I began to think I had done heretical damage and to yearn for an absolving thunderbolt. I made one of those little hitching gestures that one makes when one is trying to get oneself off one's own hook, and I cleared my throat placatingly.

He just sat there, rubbing his ear, and then he said, "As I understand it, you are asking me if I regard hopefulness as a sign of insensitivity."

Right, old boy! I thought. Right, Old Brain Trust!

"No," he said firmly. "I don't."

Well, that was great. That put period, full stop, to the whole conversation. At least, I had what I had come for—the knowledge that Detective Sloan had visited here and the even less welcome knowledge that something was certainly going on around Mig. As to hope, it was a subject on which I had nothing further to say. Tell it to old Pollo! Tell it to Anna! Tell it to the street, go sing it on the mountain! Lawd, Lawd, they's a golden house in the sky.

I mumbled something about having to go. He stood up (slowly, and I remembered with vague compunction that his bones were old) and put his hand on my arm. "Do you think I should tell Detective Sloan about the church?" he asked, and he sounded anxious.

I said "No." And he nodded. And I left. And now we are bound together, because we are both assuming a kind of responsibility that we ought not to assume, covering up for a stupid kid who isn't worth it, and we are taking the kind of chance that my Foundation pays me not to take. They would call it bad judgment.

And Father Bailey, by the echo in my ears, would call it hope.

And I, who am so recognizably romantic, call it fear. Because I do not think that my one finger in the dike will hold back the drowning waters that I am so helplessly sure will overwhelm Mig and kill Anna. If I could believe in something usable, I would ask It not to let it happen.

As it is, I shall go to bed and listen to the late and probably grim news on my radio. The last words I hear are endlessly the same: "We will be here in the morning to bring you all the news as it happened during the night." Comfortable on my pillow, in this modern world of too much communication, I can tune in the day's tragedies and terrors, alpha and omega, light foot and heavy heart, all across this globe which comes to me by courtesy of its spoilers.

What I need is a girl in my bed, not a radio by it. I wonder if the Foundation would frown on a Jeannie in my expense account? Some time I will look up Jeannie's number, some time I will call her. She seems so fresh in my mind, right now, like a meadow.

Why did I think Father Bailey was going to comfort me? At least, I am cured of any wish to go back to him.

10

Mig said, very sharply, "Anna! I have a present for you."

He stood in the doorway, holding in his arms the portable television set, fresh from the ravaged outlet store, fresh from Ernie's success and his own churchly petition. He had not meant to give it to Anna, but she was curled up against the wall, at the far corner of the bed, and he suddenly wanted to rouse her. He wanted her to come out of that haziness which seemed to cloud all her movements these days. She had glazed eyes like some stupid animal, and sometimes, at night, she got up and walked the room, very quiet so as not to wake him. But he always did wake, and he would lie listening as long as he could stand it, until at last he would hear himself yelling at her to come back to bed. And, always obedient, she would come.

"Anna!"

She rolled over and looked at him dully, and he said, half-coaxing, half-uneasy, "Anna. A present."

He sat on the bed and put the box down between them, wrenching apart the wire staples and forcing open the cardboard lid. She leaned over to see what was inside, and her heavy lids came up softly, amazed, so that she seemed quite alive and like herself. "For me?"

He was sorry at once that he had said so. He had been

tricked into giving it to her, and for a moment he was angry. Then the anger left him in an all-powerful feeling of benevolence, very heady. He leaned back, looking at her large eyes and small face, feeling himself the king that he knew he was meant to be. "You like it?" he said, very casually.

She rowed herself on her elbows, awkwardly, to the edge of the bed and sat up so that she could reach the box. He helped her pull the set out and, when it was actually free of its wrappings, shiny and very new on top of the old bed, she drew in her breath and held her hands spread out as if it was some magic fire and could warm her.

After a moment, she said, very shyly, "Now you'll stay home?" and, after another moment, he answered with a nod that surprised him. But it was true enough. The TV set would be something different from the street, or the movies, or the many drifting places that came and went with his comings and goings. If for a moment he thought it might give her a new kind of hold on him, he shrugged the idea off. He was as free as always. If he left her some day, she could creep home to that mother of hers and would not need a TV set. She would still need him, of course, but she would be able to do nothing about it, and again he had that fierce feeling of arbitrary power.

He watched her stroke the box but, when she reached to twist the dials, he snatched her hand away and said "Anna, no!" as if she was a misbehaving animal. The TV set was his, even if he had said it was hers, and he did not choose to have her using it without his permission. At the back of his head, there lay an odd disturbing picture—how she might lie on the bed, alone in the room, when he was not there, listening and watching all by herself, learning things that he did not know and discovering worlds that he did not live in. No, she would watch it with him, or not at all. He said so, and she agreed instantly and drew back a little.

He unwound the electric cord and began to examine it

carefully along its length as if he knew a great deal about electricity, impressing her. Then, whistling through his teeth, he looked around the room, choosing the right place to put it. It was then that he realized that the only outlet was the one on the ceiling, holding a single ugly bulb. The cord of the TV would not possibly reach it. He swore, loudly.

"Something?" she said anxiously.

"Nothing." He knew less about electricity than a baby would, and awareness of his ignorance made him ashamed, and shame made him angry. He would have to get hold of Ernie whose fault it all was. Ernie should have brought a longer cord from the store; Ernie had told him there was plenty of time to be choosy. "Picked you a real baby doll," Ernie had said, and then he had laughed the sickly spluttery laugh that Mig particularly disliked.

He stood, glaring, with the cord in his hand. He supposed they could unscrew the light bulb, get a long cord, and watch TV in the dark. People in real apartments and houses had outlets all over the place for the TV sets they bought (he was already thinking of the set as bought and paid for, like other people's) while he had only a hole in the ceiling through which electricity came and about which he knew nothing. He could learn, though. He could learn anything he chose to learn, and some day he would do that and he would show them all he could not be pushed around.

In the meantime, he had no way to answer Anna who was looking at him and who also knew that he could do nothing, though she would die before she said so. "There's a couple of things I have to fix up," he said defensively, "before you can see the pictures on it. Like the—" He searched his mind and came up with, "Like the battery."

She smiled, marveling at his intelligence.

"Tomorrow I'll fix that," he told her. He thought heavily how it would be to climb on the chair, hook, unhook, rehook, whenever they wanted to watch the TV, and he wondered if it might be easier just to live in the dark all the time. Hook and unhook and rehook, climb on the chair, climb down, climb up again. Nothing went right. He could have learned about electricity easily, if only someone had ever given him a chance. Then he wouldn't have to go to whiny Ernie, slip-through-a-keyhole little thief, to ask him how to hook up the stinking thing before he could even show one picture to Anna. Nobody cared whether he, Mig, ever knew anything or not. I could be a rat, he thought. I could just be a rat for all anybody cares.

He looked at Anna with dislike, and for a moment his body lurched toward her, thinking to take it out on her in the only way he knew. He didn't, because—of all the stupid, baby things to be doing—she was down on her knees with her arms around the blank, blind face of the stolen television set, and she was crying like God and Holy Mary and all the angels had come to her in a vision.

And what had happened to Anna was that Mig had given her something.

He could just give her something else too, he told himself, swaggering in his head because his body had already turned against the idea. He could just give her something else. He could show her what a man was.

Only first he would go and find Ernie and tell him what kind of a frig he had been to steal the set and not the hook-up for it. Ernie would come and find a way of fixing it, and then he, Mig, and she, Anna, would lie on the bed afterwards and watch the set that he had got for her.

He looked at Anna crying, and he felt like God. He walked out of his room, away from his TV set and his girl, and he found Ernie right away, camped on the curb and waiting to be given a bone.

Ernie said yeh-yeh, what he needed was a two-way socket,

and he would pick one up. He meant this quite literally—pick it up in his clever toothpick fingers. He knew the place to go, and he would carry it out inside his sweater, which was why he always wore a sweater two sizes too large for his skinny frame. Better than his word, he turned up within the hour, bearing not only the two-way socket but a length of electric cord and a flashlight which he did not mention because he wanted to keep it for himself.

He grinned at Anna with his bad teeth, and then he stood on the chair and made his electric bridge, while Mig watched jealously and told himself that it was an easy job and that any fool could do it. He felt injustice building up inside him.

He wouldn't let Ernie show him how to tune the dials, and he sat on his heels in front of the set and played with it until finally he got a clear picture on the lighted screen and a clear voice to go with it. The picture was a dame in a clean kitchen yakking about how good her clothes smelled. Ernie splattered the screen with his wet laugh, and Anna gave a little cry and wiped the droplets off with her fingers. Mig began to laugh too, feeling good again. It was funny, maybe. Anyway, something was funny—that dame talking about her smells, and him owning a TV set with a dame like that on it. Belonging to him.

But then, just before he left, Ernie went to the box the set had come in and hunted inside until he found a shiny-covered pamphlet. "Here," Ernie said, handing it over. "Anything you got to know, you look inside."

Mig took the manual and looked through it carefully, pretending that he knew everything it said. He could read about two words out of five, and the words he could read weren't words that told him anything. When he got to the last page, riffling through, he turned casually back to an earlier one, as if he'd missed something important. Then he nodded and started to hand it over to Ernie.

Ernie shook his head and backed off. "It's yours, Mig, comes with the set." They stood and looked at each other, and each of them knew the other's ignorance as well as he knew his own. Whatever was inside the printed pages, it was no good to them.

The picture on the TV screen had changed, and now there were four men, sitting in a row, even stiffer than the chairs they sat on. A bunch of creeps, jawing each other about something, but their words were at least words and made some sense, like street talk.

Mig's hands clenched around the manual, wanting to tear it in shreds and stuff it down Ernie's skinny craw. Then he relaxed and turned to Anna. "Here," he said generously, "this is for you," and, into her trustful hands, he put the useless, agonizing and incomprehensible paper words. She took the manual gratefully and held it to her like it was a doll.

11

I have just been through a day when everything seemed ridiculous.

I started it—ridiculously—by dodging around a corner on what is, after all, my own street when I saw Detective Sloan. I acted on a very unsound instinct, since anything that dodges is certain to rouse a cop's professional interest. I presume it did so in this case because the son of a bitch doubled back on his tracks and, when I turned the next corner, whistling and clever as a bird, there he was coming toward me again. God forbid that I should ever undertake a life of crime! The first keen and lawful eye would turn my knees to water; I would roll over like a pup, paw protecting belly.

In the few seconds before Sloan and I were nose to nose (his, hard; mine, very soft), I had ample opportunity, so fleetly flowed my brain, to philosophize that the surest way to reduce crime is to educate the imagination. My own good citizenship may be nothing more than a capacity to foresee painful consequences, and in this case, of course, my conscience was clouded. I foresaw that Sloan was going to ask me about Mig.

So I took the initiative and said jauntily, "Good morning. You're just the man I want."

He said good morning and looked out at me from under his heavy eyebrows. A detective really ought not to have such

60

heavy brows. A detective ought to have a face like a dish of oatmeal, not memorizable, looking exactly like any other dish of oatmeal. The eyebrows made me uneasy, but I was stuck in my canny conversation now and no way out. I said, though less jauntily, "Do you believe that imagination forestalls crime?"

He said "Of course" in a matter-of-fact way which annoyed me profoundly. I had not supposed he would even get my point, but I remembered that the City Fathers are now training up the gendarmerie to go to college. This is bitterly unfair to the landed gentry, the lads like me who do not expect the common man to know anything. It then occurred to me that Sloan probably thought I was talking about the policeman's imagination, not the criminal's, and I felt better, though still watchful. I wished mightily to be rid of his company but I wished even more mightily to know what he was doing in the district again. I thought of asking him, but I was afraid that he would tell me.

"See you," he said vaguely, lifted a hand and was gone.

I stood there, egg on my face and a tear in my eye, swindled by a cop. It either meant that he was no longer interested in Mig, or that he already had him in his pocket. Reason told me the former; guilt, the latter. I had a feeling that Father Bailey and I were conspiring to conceal evidence, and this unholy covenant with the Church did little to comfort me.

Tail tucked between my legs, I continued on my errand, an artless social call upon the Ruiz family who live graciously, seven in two stinking rooms, with an eighth unborn but imminent. The Ruiz family is caught up in a very ancient web known as seedtime and harvest, and the kids crawl on rotting linoleum like the cockroaches that crawl alongside them. God knows Mrs. Ruiz tries hard, but, unluckily, Mr. Ruiz tries harder. The only person who approved of Mrs. Ruiz's fruitfulness was Jeannie, who liked her so much that she felt she ought to be reproduced.

I am being ritualistically funny about all this, I see. What is it really like to be Mrs. Ruiz—to live in two rooms with that swarm of life, and none of it very healthy, and to carry in your womb still another life, and not to have any defense or hope or even that kind of grand despair that education and literature armor you with? Or did Jeannie see something that I don't see? Or did Jeannie see nothing and, as with Detective Sloan, I have misinterpreted her?

It is almost a year now since she left, my only-yesterday Jeannie, and until this past month or two I never really missed her. She is probably married, with twins, living in a two-story house with a yard in Queens. There is an old woman in the same building as the Ruiz family, who used to live in Queens but who came here, like an alley cat, when she had learned to embrace the bottle too tenderly and to be cruel to her grand-children. She is not cruel to anybody at all any more, sitting vacantly by her window, her red face fallen in like a demolished building, full of despair and banishment. Mrs. Ruiz hates her, and probably with cause, but sometimes it seems to me that living with hate across the hallway must affect the woman as much as the whiskey she drinks. Whiskey warms, so perhaps hate is worse.

Maybe what I don't like is having Mrs. Ruiz be a hater, because for a long time I saw Mrs. Ruiz as a flowering weed, rather splendid and wild and able to encompass anything. She has, incidentally, been given enough birth-control information to dam up countless generations. I don't know what she does with all the apparatus and/or pills showered on her in this Age of Revision. Maybe she has rummage sales every fourth Wednesday. If Jeannie had not left us all to fend for ourselves, I could set her to investigating the mystery. It is not, I feel, in Detective Sloan's line. Perhaps Father Bailey knows, but perhaps not, since I assume that the Ruiz family is Catholic, although there are no chromo bleeding-hearts on the wall, no crucifixes. If there ever were any, they have fallen off now along with most of the paint, that greening paint which nearly killed one of the Ruiz children. The two-year-old boy ate peeling paint to supplement . . . a diet . . . which is . . . below . . . subsistence level . . .

in-the-richest-country-in-the-world

Maybe ridiculous isn't the word for my day. Maybe sickening is.

Oh, I don't know. If the master of the Ruiz household isn't ridiculous, nothing fits the word. He sticks up in tufts like a badly-mowed lawn, and he talks incessantly in two languages, one of which is mine but neither of which can I understand. I say yes and no, almost certainly in the wrong places, and I have probably committed myself and the Foundation to unutterable and expensive acts. Ruiz is, however, alive. All of them are alive, unlike the alcoholic from Queens who died before she came here. She belongs to Father Bailey, luckily, and not to me. I have seen him knock at her door, although I have never seen her come to let him in. But then I wouldn't, would I? since I am easily dismayed by the clergy on their rounds.

I expect Father Bailey would be equally dismayed by me—sitting here, hitched to my typewriter, writing so neatly, pausing to approve felicitous bits of phrasing, here a profundity, there a witticism, all together now, boys, Professor Blount is watching! . . . . . .

Six dots. Six easy pearls to indicate an unmotivated transition.

I got nowhere with my visit to the Ruiz household. I was trying to make an agency referral, which is a delicate business for anyone in my position since we are supposed to provide direction with a delicately pointing finger, and what I generally provide is cash on the nail, wrenched from my soft heart and very difficult to account for in my Reports. . . . Come to think of it, the motivation for that transition was an emotional

one: despair. The despair was born of the fact the twenty dollars Mrs. Ruiz screwed out of me was what she had wanted in
the first place, and it was fifteen dollars more than I meant to
give her. (They're afloat, at least. Their neighbor from
Queens is not. I saw her drowned face at her dirty window.)
The motivation for my next sequence—going downtown to the
Foundation office, on an invented errand—is also despair. I
had a sudden craving for antiseptic chromium and glass and
steel, well-tended desks, well-fed carpets, all dead enough not
to feel me and alien enough so that I would not feel them.
Up here, the streets are dust and they get into everything; Park
Avenue is rock and it closes you out.

But, when I got there, onto that rich avenue which I hold in
such contempt, I did not go to the Foundation offices at all but
wandered around like a child in a Painted Desert of smooth
woods and shining metals, licking contentment with my forked
lizard-tongue in a country where no one knew me.

So, of course, for the sins of my happy self, I ran into John
Coddington Woodhill, known to the friends of his college
days as Codd. Codd is already on his way to becoming a fi-
nancial giant, and his interest in girls—which in college was
intense—is now boundless. One cannot but admire the man,
although it is difficult to see how he works them all in. By ap-
pointment? He dictates in bed? At any rate, he seems able to
combine both vocations to his own satisfaction, and, moreover,
he has married himself to a nice girl who went to Bryn Mawr.
Personally, I have always been a little awed by him, ever since
the day I saw him use a ten-dollar bill as a bookmark. Later,
I realized that a bookmark which simply happened to cost ten
dollars would not impress me at all, but of course it's the flair
that counts. That flash of coins, that ripple of paper money,
that look of a smoking wallet.

Anyway, he seemed pleased to see me this afternoon. Although I have failed to fulfill my early promise ("Couldn't sell

his novel, poor devil") I have compensated somewhat for my failure by living an exotic ghetto life. Codd regards this as a sound arrangement and respects me for having achieved it. The first thing he said to me today (looking extremely hearty, groomed, swaddled in stocks and bonds) was "How's everything? Still doing good works?"

What is there about being accused of doing good works that is so insulting? One denies it instantly. I mumbled something to the effect that the Foundation had given me a raise (not true, but a barrier between me and the Virtuous Life) and Codd said promptly, "We'll drink to that" and hustled me into a bar. Another curious thing about Codd is that, no matter where he is standing, there is always a bar at his elbow. A bar or a girl.

We groped our way through the traditional murk, and Codd, inevitably, greeted the bartender as Mac. The bartender beamed at him and swiped the bar obsequiously; if I had called him Mac, he would have thrown his wet rag in my face. (Oh, what the hell! maybe his name *is* Mac.) Codd ordered a bourbon and water, and I nodded ditto although it was not what I wanted. I sat on my high stool and felt just old enough for pink lemonade. It was that remark about doing good works that had diminished me so. I wanted to trumpet my impressive sins, but none of them was that impressive or that sinful. I am out of touch.

Codd said, "Tell me everything you've been doing. God, it's been a long time! Are you still living in that dump?" and his eyes were on a dark-haired girl, pretty as a witch, three elbows away. His bourbon slid to him decorously from the bartender's hand; I had to reach for mine. We raised glasses, nodding good health and long life to each other, and all the time he was looking at the girl. She flicked an indifferent glance at him, lit a cigarette—and looked back again. I was in a mood to believe that all his tales were true.

Since she had looked again, he was no longer interested, and I got his full attention. He gave me some very useful tips on the stock market, it never having occurred to him that the first item an investor needs is money. When I pointed this out, the bourbon stirring in my blood, he gave me a smile of surpassing sweetness and said, "Well, I suppose you have something there" as if I had offered him a revealed truth. There was a pregnant pause, and then he said, "Still writing?"

My stirring blood congealed. I said, "Yes," coldly, and I added, icily, "When I have the time."

"There's money in writing," he observed graciously. Mind you, this is a man who inherited a fortune, wrung by his ancestors from the sweating souls of peasant laborers. I hoped that the bartender's name was not Mac and that he had slipped something beside ice cubes into Codd's drink. It is infamous to be accused of writing for money when you cannot sell anything you have written.

"Sir?" said that damned bartender with just the right amount of deference.

"The same.—Richard?"

I finished my drink in one gulp and said "The same" hastily with what breath was left to me. I can hold my liquor pretty well, but I cannot swallow it fast. In the really profound silence which followed, while I fought off death by strangulation, Codd said happily, "Well, and how's your private life?" his voice nudging me in the ribs.

We both knew just what he meant, didn't we, us naughty boys. I was sorry not to be able to offer anything really fruity. My life is not so constricted as to be monastic, but I was never able to mow down those ripe and lovely fields in which Codd has always sported. The brunette, three elbows away, was inspecting him around the edge of the man next to her—a displaced person with a flat, taffy-colored face who kept sucking on a swizzle stick and looking at her. Understandably.

"Nice little dish," said Codd approvingly, not apparently looking at anything but his second drink—talented man. "You free Friday? I'm throwing a brawl."

One cannot help loving the Codds of this world. They "throw brawls" as if they were giant football players. I cleared my still-burning throat and said I was sorry, tied up, urgent matters. Predictably, he winked, generously assuming the worst. I tried unsuccessfully to look very secretive as would become a literary man. Either that second bourbon was more powerful than the first, or else I am out of practice, brooding frugally among my beer cans.

He said suddenly, "What was the name of that kid who used to work up there with you? Joan? Janet?"

"Jeannie," I said dully. "She left almost a year ago."

"Nice little dish," said Codd, and added gallantly, "No place for a woman."

I thought of Mig's little Anna. I thought of Mrs. Ruiz and of the old wreck from Queens. I thought of all the good mothers who raised good families up there, in the eye of the storm and of the Devil himself. It was, indeed, no place for a woman, and this, I thought, was no place for me. I lifted myself off my stool and said, "I have to get to the Foundation Office, Codd. It's been good to see you, and thanks for the drink."

"Sure, sure, old boy." His voice sounded heavy as if he were sleepy, which he was not, and he was looking right past the man with the taffy-colored face, right around that thin slack body. "I'll have another, I think. Call me up sometime, Richard, we'll have dinner at my club."

Is it charm? I wondered. Or does she smell the money? I touched his shoulder and he looked up, and, all of sudden, under that fogged look, there was a bright shoot of something that might yet grow if it knew where the sun was.

Well, it's not here, I thought, and I groped my way out, feeling very old old-boy indeed.

12

Anna carefully put the television book away with the copy of the women's magazine, since both of them were presents from Mig. He was aware of this, and it pleased him enough to make him remember the cross on a chain he had mentioned so fluently to Mr. Harris. If it had been anything but a cross, he would have told Ernie to pick it up, but Mig's holy relationships were working very well and he had no mind to endanger them. Father Bailey's headquarters had done him good service on the TV set; if there was to be a cross on a chain, he would, reluctantly, have to buy it.

In the end, he did not quite fulfill this pledge. He had gone into Woolworth's for an electric light bulb, because the TV set had aroused in him a latent landlordism and he believed that, if the overhead bulb burned out, the set would go black too. (He could not check this theory with Ernie because he wholly resented Ernie's superior knowledge in the matter.)

Warm in Woolworth's interior, strolling down narrow aisles between lavish counters, he came upon a display of religious items—crucifixes, crosses, statuettes of the Holy Family, rosaries—and he remembered his half-promise.

He leaned over the counter, lifted a thin gold chain and studied its tiny paper price-tag. The cross was almost as tiny as the tag, and, whatever its relation to Jesus Christ (known to be poor), it demeaned Mig's picture of his own generosity. He lifted another, larger, more beautiful, bright with a glass-diamond teardrop. It was two dollars and forty-nine cents, in this falsely nickel-and-dime place, and Anna was not worth it. He weighed it idly in his hand, trying to be contemptuous of its glitter and of the fine gold links that clung to his fingertips.

He glanced up the counter. A skinny salesgirl, red hair massed and lips like pale pewter, was poking around among the earrings, her long pointy fingers turning them over and over like jeweled bugs, but she was not looking at him. Nobody was looking at him, and once more he was swept by the conviction that, to everyone else's eyes, he simply did not exist. He could do whatever he wished to do, because nobody cared.

The chain and its winking cross fitted perfectly into the palm of his hand. His fingers closed around it, and his hand moved discreetly to his pocket. The two-dollar-and-forty-nine-cents treasure slid, smooth-linked, bright-diamond-glassed, into his possession.

He stood there for a moment, leaning a little further over the counter as if he were making some very delicate selection, then he straightened up. Between his shoulders, he could feel eyes like a knife, but, when he turned around, there was no one there. The salesgirl's fingers were still fiddling the earrings, and he wondered how much jewelry she took home with her at night, stuffed down the front of her dress, high in her stocking behind a skinny knee. Everybody took everything they could lay their hands on. Only he—

He felt a cold shiver run straight down him, from the place between his shoulders where the knife-eyes had rested, to the heels of the new shoes that had been stolen for him. That was the one rule he had meant never to break, the rule he had always kept in a world where theft was more common than garbage: never to steal the thing itself, always to let someone else do it for him.

But this had been so easy, it had seemed like it was meant. And he would not do it again, only this once for Anna. He pictured her gratitude when he dropped it from his cupped hand into hers, and he swore to himself that this would be the last, the only time. Let him just get to the door and outside on the street, let Ernie be the one to get into trouble forever after this.

There was a man moving steadily toward him, big-handed like a cop. Mig went stiff.

If he got picked up for one little steal like this, his own nice clean hands—for the first, unclever time—would no longer be nice and clean. Mr. Harris would find out, and that creeping detective, and everything for Mig would be entirely different. He cursed Anna inside his head, Anna who had got him into this trap, and he started toward the street door, trying desperately not to run and so give himself away hopelessly but finding his trapped thoughts running faster and faster and his trapped feet fighting him to run with his thoughts and knowing that, if he once let himself run . . . .

At the door, he looked back. The man had turned down another aisle and was moving heavily in the opposite direction. Every ounce of fear slid off Mig's sweating body, and his scared heart slowed down. He was king again. He gave a short, hard, happy laugh and put his hand down into his pocket, rubbing the cross between his fingers as if it was a lucky piece.

Which maybe it was. But, next time, it would be Ernie's feet that did the running and Ernie's heart that shook in his throat. He had enough on Ernie-boy to tie him up forever, and the principles of economic enterprise were not lost on Mig.

He walked home, smiling. But, when he came into the room, there was Anna crouched over a bowl, being sick. Her dark hair was whipped damp across her sallow forehead, and her eyes peered through the strands like an alley cat's. He stood silent in the doorway and he looked at her and he hated her. She saw his eyes and she shrank tinier than ever and made a whimpering sound, pushing the bowl away as if it should not be there. He kept on staring at her with a sort of torn disgust, and he thought resentfully that he had brought her a beautiful gift and risked himself doing it and all she could do was be sick like an animal.

Her hand was shaking. She lifted it and pushed her hair back and took a long breath and said she was all right. She said, through heavy breathing, that she had eaten some sausage, it must have been bad, she was all right now.

He wanted to believe her. He did believe her. She looked better under his very eyes, and when she stood up and walked over to sit on the edge of the bed, she walked straight enough. To show his relief, he touched her shoulder. And then, to show his love of which by now he was intensely proud, he pulled the cross out from his pocket and dropped it, shining, into her lap.

She began suddenly to cry, salt tears spilling down her cheeks, past her lips, onto the stained front of her dress. She put both hands down on the cross, fingers interlaced, pressing against it, as if she was afraid it would go away. Her mouth moved.

He suspected her of praying, and, indeed, in her way, she was saying a thanksgiving grace. The foul green liquid that Mama Kraus had given her had certainly not stayed down long enough to do any good, not long enough to poison the baby who lay so deep inside. She would have to go back to Mama Kraus and her way of saying "If this don't work, there's other ways, my dear," which somehow sounded cruel instead of friendly, even though Mama Kraus always repeated how glad she was to be able to help poor girls in trouble, being a Christian herself.

But now the cross lay on Anna's lap, and the cross was certainly a sign that Jesus Christ Himself had forgiven her, and she did feel much better. It was a gift from Jesus Christ and from Mig, both the feeling-better and the beautiful cross.

Mig said, "Stop crying, Anna, you'll make yourself sick again," and she managed a smile that was tired but did not tremble too much. She lifted her hands, and there under them was the cross. She saw the diamond and the fine gold chain, and she said, "Thank you, Lord Jesus," not loud enough for Mig to hear, and "Thank you, Mary-and-Joseph."

Since, to Anna, the Holy Family always stayed the same age, the Lord Jesus to whom she offered thanks was a very small baby. The thought might have greatly amused Mama Kraus.

13

Mig has been here again, and I have been behaving like the
great-granddaddy of all mankind. Precepts and aphorisms
flowed from my lips; I was a pundit, a savant, the Seven Wise
Men of Greece discoursing as one. Alas, that I could not be
bottled, corked and stored in my vintage year.

Now, two hours later, I remember very little of what I said,
only the heady excitement of saying it. I certainly urged Mig
to make something of himself, to be good to Anna (he says
that she was sick the other day, but is better now; he says he *is*
good to her). I certainly urged him to leave these streets and
become a man, to breathe fresh air. I waved my hand downtown toward Manhattan's libraries and museums, his for the
asking, knowing perfectly well that he cannot even read
properly and that his idea of art is graffiti on a subway wall. I
commended to him all the distant beauties of life; I suggested
his going back to school. I even offered to get him a job downtown, confidently promising that John Coddington Woodhill
will hire an uneducated ghetto nonentity with no skills and
no observable ambition.

Mig listened, which of course is why I talked so much.
Hungry dog, he lapped me up. Or, clever weasel, he pretended
to. My high-minded, rational and well-expressed advice should
have transformed his life; my noble thoughts were more than

73

adequate to usher in the millennium. Dazzled by my own rhetoric, I said goodnight to him as if he were my brother. And now I am sitting at this typewriter, and my golden zeal has turned into a handful of ashes. (There's a metaphor for you, minted fresh from pure tin.)

The truth is, I do not really like Mig. I even have moments of hating him. I want to reform him, and I know I am not fit to give him the advice I gave tonight. Cock of the world two hours ago, I can only sit here now and feel depressed and ashamed.

Perhaps it's just the time of night, and the weather which is turning colder, with all that means in this ugly part of an ugly world. Dark nights that old eyes stare into, cold beds that cold children lie in, ice and snow, daggers and stabbings and shootings, piteous cries to the Department of Health for more heat and to God for more light.

I don't understand. I do *not* understand. I was so full of good intentions when I came to this street. I thought that I would write great books and that I would serve my fellow man. Instead, I seem to have become a sort of court jester, exhorting Mig to all the things he should do and see and be, but never taking my own good advice. The paintings in the museums, the books, the symphonies, the lovely animals in the zoo. The girls I could hold. The children I could have. And I just crouch here, like all the others, four walls to a room and a dark street outside.

I suppose what I thought, three years ago, was that I would move graciously into this world and enlarge it for its inhabitants. Instead, it has conspired to grow around me, and I have shrunk. The meanest of my neighbors seems rather better than I am—since, after all, the advantages are entirely on my side, or so my civilized and college-privileged brain informs me.

Now that I have written my novel and shelved it, will I shrink away entirely, turn into a ghetto lapdog, offering Foun-

dation funds in exchange for kind words and a pat? Or is it
stubbornness that keeps me here, a determination to make sense
of things? A curious project for these parts. Sense is our scarcest
commodity.

I can document that.

Item. Cassy is actually going to a secretarial school. Illiterate
and ignorant little mule that she is, she sits four hours a day in
a classroom, a Place of Learning no less, where she applies the
touch system and pothooks to words that she can neither spell
nor understand. At night, she passes on to Irmalee what she
has learned by day, since only one of them can afford to go.
Cassy now says that Angel found the money, and I know that
the word "found" is a euphemism but there is nothing I can
do about it. I wonder what Angel does at night while Cassy
tutors Irmalee in their curiously shared room. How do the
lessons come out, stumbling first in Cassy's mind and then
stumbling again in her girl friend's? I ache, thinking of them,
and this conditioned reflex is the sum total of my contribution
to their futures. But, while I ache, they move. They *will* get on.
While I nuzzle the dead carcass of my aborted career, leave my
books unopened on my shelves, smother Mig in my own unreal-
ized dreams, Cassy and Irmalee are sailing straight into the
eternal winds on Angel's dowry.

Item. Mrs. Detty rose from a sickbed today to appear in
court and testify to the good character of a drug addict. She
put her best hat on to cover her fever and told me that she was
planning perjury. Her client is thirty years old, and he is
supporting a manageable drug habit, a wife and two children
(or is it two wives and one child?). He is terrifyingly polite
because he walks a tightrope of sanity, and Mrs. Detty says that
he steals a little but she knows who he steals from and she
makes it up to them. I used to think that, if the City knew
what was going on in Mrs. Detty's devious administration, they
would fire her out of hand. But now I am convinced that the

75

City does know, and that this is exactly the way in which things are kept going. Jugglers with a hundred balls in the air must not be interrupted during the performance of their act. Mrs. Detty's husband was a construction worker who died fifteen years ago in an unnecessary accident, for which his widow received minimum compensation. They had no children. But now she has a dozen husbands and wives, a hundred brothers and sisters, aunts and uncles, grandparents and great-grandparents, a thousand babies of all sexes and colors, all without apparent end. She tells me, at least once a month, that if she could only write, she would write a book about the things she sees. She also tells me her dreams which are no duller than most people's, and she has been thinking of crocheting me a necktie but, thank God, has found neither the time nor her crochet hook. I could cut my heart out for Mrs. Detty and lay it at her feet, but I sense she would not regard this as a useful gesture.

Item. The wild black giantess, with five children in two rooms, has just removed herself and her unholy joy from our midst. She will be back in two weeks. It is that time of year for her when, like a serpent sloughing its skin, she goes off alone on what she describes as a "journey." Fourteen days and God only knows how many gallons of gut-whiskey later, she will come back to us, sober, chilled, monumental as if she had held her head among stars. After one night in her own bed, blanketed with children, she will rise again, totally herself, gorgeous, jovial, yeasty with life, booming her splendid obscenities and pinning me down with a damp child on each knee while she tells me, in loving and exact detail, her plans for feeding the landlord on rat poison. (I have seen a rat come out of her wall and then scuttle back when she glared at it. When I first knew her, I thought she was a genuine hex woman, but now I have come to believe that she has something on the rats and they know it.) All her u's are oo's, and she talks to me about my Ooniversity where she is planning to send her oldest boy. Her oldest boy is just twelve, a fourth-grade dropout and barely able to read street signs, but, curiously enough, he works very dependably for a grocer and I am already resigned to the thought that, some day, he will own the establishment. Who needs to read, born of a mother who can blackmail rats?

Item. A man, whose name is Lonergan or Longan or Logan or London, asks me at intervals to stop by and help him with his "papers." He is a strange, little creature, dried up and blinking, with the kind of face that shows the grinning skull behind the skin and the skin is leather. He lives in a hole that would be an indecency in any country, any civilization, and he spends most of his Welfare checks on postage stamps and envelopes so that he can enter the contests from which, some day, he intends to make his fortune. He exists in continuous expectation of a shower of gold, of a sky-blue sports car, or a tour to the Bahamas, all expenses paid. He labors over the coupons, muddling them sometimes almost beyond repair with the pitiful fumblings of his soft black pencil and the labored exorcism of his dirty eraser. He does them wrong over and over again, sure that he can do it himself, and it is only occasionally that he gives up on the most difficult cases and asks my advice, as if I were his lawyer. I have learned to carry a red ballpoint pen with me so that my writing will show up through the thicket of his thumbprints, and I have also learned to wait patiently on his decision whether to sign himself Lonergan or Longan or Logan or London. The other names, of course, are aliases. I understand that his miscellaneous prison terms were for counterfeiting; he was bound to be caught under any alias, incompetent to the end. In any event, he has won three genuine prizes: a gold-filled lapel pin, a month's supply of cat food (he ate it), and a certificate which entitles him to a fifteen-dollar rebate on a twelve-volume encyclopedia. When he finally wins his fortune, he says he will buy a stucco house in Florida and live there until he dies. He will also take up golf. I nod approval, knowing that all this is merely his survival kit. Without it, he could not get through a single jungle night.

Which raises an interesting question. If this is a jungle, what are all these middle-class people with their middle-class ambitions doing here? Romantic that I am, it has taken me a long time to realize that many of my neighbors in these God-forsaken streets are hopelessly middle-class, or want to be. Cassy and Irmalee yearn only to better themselves, to become little American minnows in the great pool of American commerce where all their color will wash away. (And that contrast of color—all black, all white—seems so startling and beautiful to me, but of course I can afford to be aesthetic about colors. I am not trapped by my skin.) My black giantess only seeks a world where her children, one by one, will go to college, although it is highly problematical whether any of them will even reach eighth grade. She never asks if the college curriculum is relevant. Only college students and their professors can afford the luxury of that kind of question. Here, relevance is the next meal.

As for Lonergan-Longan-Logan-London, what can be more middle-class than his dream of the Bahamas and the sky-blue car? All he wants is the Gold Rush and the Rainbow's End, the American Dream itself, and his counterfeiting and embezzling were meant to serve as a short-cut. Just as Mrs. Detty's pathetic addict only wants to live an adjusted family life. It happens that he adjusts on heroin, but it is only a metered adjustment, enough to pull him through one dawn and on to another.

The one properly middle-class personality up here ought to be Mrs. Detty herself. Sociologically and census-wise, she is middle-class to her backbone. She was, however, born to be either a peasant, a duchess or God. If she was God, she would pass a host of very simple miracles, the kind that a free-enterprise, democratic government ought to be able to pass automatically. Cassy and Irmalee would find good jobs, the giantess's children would go to college, and Lonergan-Logan would have a house of his own and a color TV set. Everybody would be happy.

I see, however, that I am making everything rather too simple. What I have left out of my excellent thesis on middle-class values is any mention of fear. Fear is something that the people up here live with all the time, dawn, noon and black night. The middle-class may scare themselves with ghost stories and headlines, but they do not really live with the knife at the throat, the sound at the door, the mugger in the hallway, the driftwood bodies of winos and junkies, the police siren, the scream, the flame, the thud. The middle-class come here to visit, to inspect or even to live (as I, middle-class I, have come) but they—we—come with protective equipment, first-aid kits, compasses, beaters to go through the high grass ahead of us, financed by Foundations and secure in the knowledge that the natives will welcome our small band of enlightened, high-minded and colonizing sahibs.

So I avoid too much thinking about my neighbors by writing about them as if they were merely quaint characters, a little dangerous, eminently colorful, highly picturesque.

One thing I have learned. Anything is picturesque, if you can leave it. And this, of course, is the fundamental weakness of my position here. I can leave. I can leave any time I want to.

But not yet. Not yet a while.

14

He would not do it again and the stolen cross still burned fire in the palm of his hand, but he was pleased with her pleasure. He bragged about it to Ernie, carefully suppressing how he had come by the cross since his arrogance would not permit Ernie and himself to operate on the same level.

Besides, he had broken his cardinal rule when he risked arrest. Ambition was Mig's shelter as much as it was his spur, and he was delicate in his maneuvers. The very ease of the theft had betrayed him, the cross moving so naturally into his hand, but he would not do it again. The act did not fit his plans for the future.

He was beginning to think that Anna did not fit his plans, either. She was sick too much of the time, mewing and meager. Her eyes grew enormous, and he could have broken her wrists between thumb and forefinger. She waited on him, bent over like an old woman. She watched television, curled against his side like a little cat. He was used to her, but unless she got better soon, she was going to turn into a dragging load. She had promised him she was not having a baby, and he believed her because he wanted to. Occasionally he estimated her waistline, but he was sexual without understanding anything about the process and his knowledge of cause and effect was exceedingly vague. He would have liked to ask Ernie some direct questions, but Ernie already knew his ignorance of the laws of electricity and Mig had no intention of giving himself away further.

He was restless, sometimes sharp. After a while, he convinced himself that Anna would be better off somewhere else. He thought he would send her back to her family. He even pictured himself giving her the TV set, which would certainly make her welcome at home, and the thought of this rather curious dowry encouraged him.

He chose bed as the place to inform her of his plans. Because he was pleased with his own solution and because, in the darkness, she seemed neither thin nor sorrowful-eyed, he laid his cheek against her hand and said "Anna" very gently.

She made the small sound that lovers make for poets.

"I've been thinking about you," he said, and the statement made him feel solid as if he weighed more than he did. "You've been sick lately—" He ignored her protest, tightening his hand on hers to keep her quiet. "It's not good for you here," he said generously. "It's time to go back to your family."

He saw, too late, how disastrously he had said it. She gave a cry of absolutely perfect happiness, like a bird at dawn, and flung herself against him. He did not know exactly what she was telling him in the broken ecstasy of her words, but he heard enough to know that she had prayed to the Blessed Virgin and that the Blessed Virgin had now answered her prayers. He heard her say that she and Mig could now go home together and live as one family. She cried a little from happiness while he lay rigid, and then she said further that they need not really be married, they only had to pretend that they were. But they would have to pretend, because—

He stopped her mouth with his hand before she could tell him what he did not want to hear, and then he told her, with a kind of frantic brutality, that he meant for her to go home alone. He did not add that he would greatly prefer to die than to face her mother, which was only a partial choice because he was convinced that her mother, given the opportunity, would most certainly kill him. He was much more afraid of women than he was of men. Of death, he was most afraid of all.

He sat up in bed and he said "I've decided" as if he were emperor of the world.

He heard in the dark a long breath, and then he heard nothing at all. He was relieved. She would go home to her mother without fuss or storm, and he would be a free man again. Perhaps now he would find the long-legged, lovely, golden-haired dream to occupy his bed. He sat there and spun out of golden hair a fantasy, under cleaner sheets and in a better world, and he became drugged and swollen and sleepy. And, being so, he turned to Anna like a baby to a bottle.

It was then that he realized how silent she was. When he reached to touch her, her hand felt clammy. Terror shrieked instantly in his mind. She was dead. He leaned to hear her breathe, and she was not breathing. He spread his fingers, which had only touched, and they shook so that he could not really feel, so that cold turned to imagined ice. His mind raced wildly ahead, disaster piled on disaster, there would be police, questions, suspicion, jail. And, somewhere in all that, he really did not want her to die. He could not survive without her comfort in all the disasters that would be caused by her death.

He filled his lungs with air and, yelling against fate, defiant and imploring, he shouted "Anna!" and she sat up.

She sat up alive, faintly visible in the dark room against the dark window. She breathed, she moved, she spoke, and nothing was dead but her voice. She said "Mig."

He was too flooded with relief to rescue himself. He believed that if he struck her down again a second time, she would surely die. He said, lamely, his lungs empty, "Forget I said anything. Forget I said anything, Anna. It was just an idea."

"Mig," she said again, and this time it was the bird voice. In the dimness, he saw her fold her hands over her breast, enclosing the cross he had given her. The room was safely empty. The arresting police, the judging courts, even Anna's mother had left it. So, alas, had the golden hair and the spun dream and the road to escape.

Anna's breath came lightly, joyously. He listened to it for a while, and then at last he shrugged his defeat and lay back on the bed. Sadly perplexed, he was a long time falling asleep.

15

Sweet Mig has been around again, this time to ask how I manage the women in my life. He talks vaguely about a blonde, which is certainly not Anna, and he inquires with a suitable hangdog look how to shake her loose.

He is, I suppose, seventeen. He has Anna, that little ewe lamb who needs all the comfort the world will never give her, and he comes scabbing to me about his other ladies. I am possessed by a frankly Victorian longing to kick him downstairs, and I am secretly embarrassed by the dabbling fingers of his curiosity. The session is neither bull, nor calf. Next time he comes here, I shall reach for my jacket and tell him firmly that I am on my way out.

The truth is, I avoid Mig lately. Not because of his garland of young women (after all, he is only Codd without Codd's money and opportunity) but because Detective Sloan has been visiting me again, and his circling questions seem to be zoning in. He isn't talking about thefts now, he is talking about that common streetware of drugs (name your poison, we have them all). If Mig is pushing drugs, I'll kill him.

. . . Down, boy. Down, dog. Down, typewriter. That's what I use this small infernal machine for: to trap my murders on paper so that no one will be hurt by them. I don't even believe my fears about Mig. From what I know of him—which is a good deal—I can't picture him taking the risk. My boy is cautious, silly, probably mean, but above everything else he is selfish, ridden by self-care and self-concern.

I am sick of him at this moment. I am sick of everything up here. I learned this afternoon that Pollo, my poor old Tom o' Bedlam, has escaped the world by dying out of it, and I hope that his pious daughter is very happy. I know that I am not, and I cannot shake him from my mind. I keep remembering the way he tried to get jobs for himself, the way he sometimes stood on the corners of silly streets selling silly fake peacock feathers—"very che'p, very very che'p." There's one on my wall now, looking at me with its peacock god-eye, its colors fraudulent, its brightness deranged by dust. I could blow the dust away, I suppose, a farewell gesture, *vale Pollo.* What I really wish is that I had bought all his che'p feathers that day just to see his eyes with some light in them.

His eye. He only had one.

Maybe I should go and talk to Father Bailey and arrange some kind of a memorial service. We could invite Pollo's daughter who committed him, and we could invite his friends. There would suddenly be a lot of them because funerals are very popular up here, and there are always more comrades for the dead than there are for the quick. (No responsibilities involved? or just a free show?) I would enjoy seeing what Pollo's daughter would make of Lonergan's skullface, of my black giantess, of Mrs. Ruiz's snotty babies (each with a cockroach in its hand; I am beginning to concoct a fantasy for revenge), of Cassy and Irmalee nuzzling their Angel between them, of that unblessed sodden damozel from Queens (the original leaned out from the gold bar of Heaven and this one leans on every bar——but I wonder if that pun is quite so funny as I thought it would be?) . . . . . Well, there is my sad silent pageant of mourners, soft-footed and gone, with Pollo's frail issue quivering in the midst of it all.

Mrs. Detty would not approve of my vendetta. She has already told me that Pollo's daughter meant well. Mrs. Detty is my conscience, my pacifier, my teething ring, she lets me hold her hand in the dark of my troubles. But what am I supposed to do?—hold my own hand, fingers clutching familiar fingers? It seems unnatural, almost incestuous, and besides Mrs. Detty's hands would be out of work.

Who holds Mrs. Detty's hand in the dark?

Father Bailey, perhaps. She talks very sweetly about Father Bailey, it's like listening to the sound of daisy chains being woven. Jeannie did that too. Women always like clergymen, women like to pretend that things are very safe.

Men invent women. For the hundredth time, I am thinking about telephoning Jeannie at the only number I have for her, but the truth is that I am afraid she is no longer there, or, worse, that she no longer remembers me. Richard? Richard *who?*

Richard Harris Richard Harris Richard Harris. Present, sir. Present, Professor Blount. Present, though not accounted for.

Who holds Father Bailey's hand?

To get back to Mig. He had two cokes and a cigarette, and then he did that curious cat-prowling of his among my things, touching the books superciliously (as if, because they are no use to him, he revenges himself with contempt) and brushing his fingers across the keys of my typewriter. Finally, when this studied performance was over, he sat on the edge of my table and asked me if I have a girl.

My old bones jumped. I dream of Jeannie, I wrestle Maxine, I am occasionally grateful to others more nameless, and once I had a Dorothy at breakfast time. She smelled deliciously of campus life and made burned toast with real charm, but I think she was doing research on the ghetto and that she wrote me up in her term paper as an Aspect of Welfare.

I made, for Mig, a sort of diffident grunt which encouraged him to tell me about his blonde, a vanilla-ice-cream bit I think he must have scooped straight out of a movie screen. I reinterpret her in my head as an obliging young neighbor who is furthering his education and who is unknown to Anna (not that Anna could or would do anything about it) and who, for public discussion, is America the Beautiful. Their nights are one prolonged swooning in the casbah. After a pause, he says that a girl like that would—wouldn't she?—would certainly know how to . . . . .

We commence a deathless dialogue.

Richard (not helpful) : How to . . . . ?

Mig: How to. Take care of herself.

Richard: But don't *you?*

Mig (frantic with wounded vanity) : Yes, of course. But this was different. She . . . .

Richard (relieved, on Anna's behalf) : Well, probably.

Mig (plainly hating me) : Probably what?

Richard (offhand and sweating) : Probably knows how to take care of herself. Good God, Mig, ask *her,* not me.

Mig (wholly reassured) : That's what I'd figured, that she'd know.

We sit there, exhausted—high-minded Knights of the Round Table, concerned only for our ladies' good. It occurs to me, uncomfortably, that Mrs. Detty would knock our heads together. I even feel a stealthy yearning to be clouted by Mrs. Detty. I would clout Mig, Mrs. Detty would clout me, and she could then be off to Mrs. Ruiz's for a nice cup of tea and, with those tongues of theirs that can flay a moose if they wish, a cozy chat about morality among young men. I can picture the two of them clearly, as I can picture the memorial for Pollo. It is my night for fantasies.

Anyway, Mig is gone now, and I am half inclined to credit the existence of his blonde. I would like to believe in her, because it would take some of the burden of Mig off Anna. She, poor baby, needs only to feed and warm and touch him and to live in his pocket and thank him for crumbs.

I feel suddenly more cheerful. I feel bright and literary and creative, a product no doubt of this typing therapy. If it were not so far past midnight, I would put a fresh page into the typewriter and begin a novel. A short story, at least. A poem?

On second thought—and on the unfaltering evidence of the beer cans in the wastebasket—I have had too much refreshment. Experience tells me that, read by daylight, the pages would flutter down, one by one, inexorably, on top of the beer cans. Observe how nimbly critical my brain is tonight. I can see the worthlessness of what I write even before I write it.

What the hell am I so scared of?

16

The conversation with Mr. Harris had ended too soon, or at any rate it had not gone in the right direction.

Anna's reassuring words had been contradicted by her continuing sicknesses, and Mig's suspicions flared up again. He was now beginning to think that she was going to have a baby but that she was too stupid to know it.

His dialogue with Mr. Harris should have been very simple, but the hoped-for word *abortion* had never been reached. Perhaps it was a word that Mr. Harris did not know, being a common street term, or perhaps his girls just never got into this kind of trouble. After all, Mr. Harris had a college education. He had simply assumed, with irritating heartiness, that Mig must know all the answers already, and the only reward that Mig had for an abrasive evening was a flickering conviction that Mr. Harris had, on the whole, been rather embarrassed.

The thought was pleasurable, but the problem was not solved. He would have to fall back, reluctantly, on Ernie, and Ernie had been missing for two days, fading into some world of his own and perhaps aware of the long shadow that was being cast by Detective Sloan. Mig's resentful inquiries brought no results, and then, out of nothing, Ernie reappeared, wearing a broad-brimmed hat snappily trimmed with leather and brass studs.

There was a self-satisfied smile on his jug-eared, hoot-owl

face, and Mig had to suppress a blind impulse to knock the hat off his silly head. "Looks like you been to Coney Island," he said coldly and had the satisfaction of seeing the hoot-owl feathers droop.

"I got it downtown," Ernie said lamely. "I didn't tell you about it, Mig, because you always say you don't want to know nothing, but it's a good place, way off, out of that fug's territory. I didn't think you wanted to know nothing more."

"Okay, okay, then shut up. If you know so much what I want, why do you keep talking?" He watched the anxious puppydog straining at its leash for a kind word and a pat, and he knew that he had the upper hand of Ernie just the way Mr. Harris had the upper hand of him. "What'd you get for *me?*"

"I didn't think you wanted a hat."

"Not that piece of cheese," Mig said contemptuously, having wanted the hat with his whole heart from the moment he saw it.

Ernie said "Yeah" on a note of real sorrow. "Tell you the truth, Mig, I didn't get nothing else. I was in this store downtown, see, and the hat was easy dirt, so I figured the whole place ought to be easy. If you can lift a hat like this one without getting a shake, you can lift an elephant."

"Looks like an elephant's hat," Mig agreed, and suddenly they both doubled over, silly with the schoolboy joke, whooping an idiot mirth. Ernie whooped just a little louder, and he stopped as soon as Mig did and said eagerly, "I can get anything there, Mig, and it's real out of our district. You name it, it's yours."

Mig shrugged and waved him silent, his mind not on merchandise. He lowered himself to the stoop, pulled a cigarette out of his pocket and scratched a match across brownstone that had once known real elegance. The street was full of garbage and kids and wreckage of all kinds, including human, but he saw nothing of it, having at the moment no need of anything it could give him. "I'll think about it," he said, and then added, very casually, very cleverly, "Ask you a question, Ernie." He yawned, establishing his indifference. "There was a thing on TV yesterday . . ."

"Your set okay?" said Ernie eagerly. (Steal you a couple of new tubes, boss? Grab you an antenna?)

"I'll tell you when it isn't." Mig scowled. If there was one thing he hated, it was to have an invented story interrupted all the time. "On TV," he said firmly, "there was this guy got a girl into trouble, and the girl was crying and carrying on about what she was going to do——" He broke off, admiring the high tone of his phrasing but not sure that Ernie would get the message.

Ernie looked at him and said "Yeah" rather cautiously.

"It was a story, like," Mig said. "Anna watches them, I don't. But the next bit she missed it, and she was asking me—"

He broke off again. There was a silence into which a police siren screamed, rose, fell and died away. Ernie, out of his clumsy head, did a great kindness. "Like Anna wants to know if this chick's going to be okay?"

Mig, who now knew that Ernie knew why he was asking, nodded. "She's only a kid," he said. "She don't understand it's just a show on TV. She thinks it's *serious*." He pulled a second cigarette out of his pocket, and this one he offered to Ernie. Ernie shook his head and produced his own, reminding Mig again of that small weakness. But, so far, the little rat had been all right, and Mig gave him the matches.

"I knocked up a girl once," Ernie said, and this was his second kindness to Mig and a bit of wishful lying. Ernie, at sixteen, was as totally pure as he was totally knowledgeable. This bothered him less than it might have as he had, by night, truly remarkable dreams and, by day, a very pretty imagination. Even now, in memory of the non-existent occasion, he was able to swagger a little.

Mig nodded, curt and male.

Ernie sagged, but at least he knew the right answer. "You tell Anna that girl on TV would go to someone like Mama Kraus. That's where *my* girl went." He thought of Mama Kraus and then he thought of small Anna, and something inside him lurched a little. But it was Anna's own fault. She soaked up Mig's time like a greedy sponge, and, besides, she was just the kind of girl he would have chosen for himself. Not for him Mig's golden blonde, just someone who was so pretty and even smaller than he was, someone who would have to look up to see his face.

He glanced at Mig, then dropped down on the stoop beside him. They sat so, legs spread, hands on knees, cigarettes dangling. He kept silence, because he could see that Mig was thinking.

"Mama Kraus," Mig said slowly. Relief possessed him. He gave a sudden yell, sprang to his feet and whacked Ernie on his shoulder. "Sure you don't want an elephant's hat?" he shouted and hurled himself, in a dizzying ballet, over, under and around the rusty iron railing that ran alongside the dirty brown steps and up to the dirty brown door.

Ernie eyed him with pride, dimly aware that he himself had wrought this wild release.

There was, after all, nothing to it. Mig was master of the situation from start to finish.

He strode into their room and he found Anna standing by the window, looking out. She had not heard him (lately, it was as if she had a sort of deafness) and he walked over, took her by the shoulders and turned her around. He said, almost amiably, "Don't lie to me about it, Anna. You're going to have a kid." He waited for her to answer, but she just lay standing against his arms. "Aren't you?" he said.

She said something then that he couldn't really hear—yes, no, maybe, how did you find out?—but it didn't matter because now he was in charge. He gave her a little shake and put her away from him, and he said to the top of her head, "It's nothing to get yourself sick about, Anna. I've been asking around for you." Lord and master and teacher and social worker, he was. "All you do is go to Mama Kraus. She'll fix you up."

He felt the movement of her all through her, up into his own hands. "You just *go* to her, Anna," he said. "It's easy."

After quite a time, she looked up.

There were two things helping her. The first was that Mig's voice was so kind, and she wasn't used to his being really kind and it was like being warm. The other thing was that maybe she'd been wrong about the green stuff that Mama Kraus had given her, the stuff that had made her so sick. Maybe it had worked, after all? "Come back if it don't help you, dear," Mama Kraus had said. "There's another way that always works." She hadn't gone back. Even to think about going back had made her sicker than the green stuff had, and anyway maybe the baby had died inside her.

That was it. The green stuff had poisoned the baby right away, like it would have poisoned her if she hadn't thrown most of it up. She said, in a very small voice, "I've been to Mama Kraus, Mig, I've already been." Her voice got a little louder. "Everything's all right now. Everything's all right."

He pulled her to him in a jubilance of relief, kissed her mouth with something that might almost be taken for love, and then let her go. "Fix it up, so you don't take no chances again, Anna," he said. Quick, neat, executive. *"No* kids. You hear me?"

She heard him. She knew she could not have the child, but neither could she face going back to Mama Kraus for that final, unspoken and terrifying act that "always worked." But perhaps what she had told Mig was true, perhaps everything really was all right?

She could do nothing except wait and, of course, pray. But when she put her hand to the cross that lay against her throat, she could not really believe that even God loved her.

17

I turned up at Father Bailey's door just as he was showing another visitor out. It was a little lizard of a man, who whisked past me and down the stairs as if I were a walking plague and who called back something over his shoulder which I could neither hear nor understand, only that the high-pitched voice was like a needle.

Father Bailey raised his hand in reply or blessing, and I thought with irritable satisfaction how convenient it must be to have the Church breathing balm over your shoulder and relieving you of personal responsibility. Unfair to Father Bailey, of course, but my mood was black.

It had been black all day—perhaps too much solitary orgy last night, typewriter and beer waltzing in each other's arms. The day itself ought to have made me feel better, and the street had a rainbow quality which I was not prepared to appreciate. There was a cat in the gutter outside my building—not a dead cat which would have matched my mood but a very alive cat, a contortionist cat with one leg wrapped around its ear and a look of blind idiot contentment. I felt that it was unnatural for a cat to be washing itself in the gutter, but then I thought that, if you are already in the gutter, no one can give you a kick and send you flying there. This bit of philosophy deepened my melancholy, and the only reason I kept on walking toward Father Bailey's was that I had made up my mind to go there.

Now the scuttling lizard on his stairs had confirmed my mood. I suddenly had no wish at all to make this clerical call, only to run back down the stairs and out of the building and into the street and out of the city, not stopping until I had found a tree and a meadow and a blue sky and a fish or a bird or a comet named Hope. The urgency of my desire was not made better by the knowledge that there is nothing and no one to stop me. I have my little savings in my little savings bank. I live in the age of jet planes; I could be in Ecuador, Tokyo, Nairobi sooner than tomorrow. The giant airlines jostle each other for my patronage, wooing me with planked salmon flown in from Scotland, prime beef from the Argentine, martinis at 30,000 feet and stewardesses like pretty doves. Westward ho!

"Yes," said Father Bailey, closing the door with me on his side of it. I took a chair and studied my knuckles. After a while, he said politely, "Is something the matter?" I wrapped my mortal shell more tightly around me, gave a bitter laugh and said "Chronic melancholia" tersely. My ears turned hot at once, the adolescent remark ringing in them.

Father Bailey examined the word *melancholia* by repeating it under his breath until it began to sound like a Latin prayer. Irritation cooled my ears, and I broke in to say that no doubt he was going to tell me that I was dramatizing myself. He said no, no indeed, as if he were declining a cup of tea, and observed that many people were drawn toward melancholy. He then added, "But one doesn't have to make human sacrifices to it, does one?"

The voice was the voice of Professor Blount, saying oh-so-nicely that colleges do not offer their writing courses for therapeutic reasons. I felt the bile run nastily for a moment, and then I dredged up my best yes-Herr-Professor smile and gave it to Father Bailey. He smiled back like a baby lamb, and I sat straighter, a good child in a hard pew. I said, "No, sir"

95

virtuously. "You are quite right," I said. "I was dramatizing myself," I said.

"Were you?" said Father Bailey, sincerely interested.

This concluded our dialogue on Melancholia. I must try the fine word on Mrs. Detty some time. She will put a patch on my injured feelings, because I am a human being and that is what Mrs. Detty does for human beings.

I said formally, "I'm keeping you from your work, Father Bailey." (I cannot call him simply Father as everyone else does on this idiot street. I have a father of my own. He lives in New Jersey and, when he introduces me to someone, he either says that I work for a Foundation or that I work in a ghetto, depending on the political and social nuances involved. He makes a very good living, selling insurance, and sometimes he is obliged to work both sides of the street—as who isn't?—but he is an honorable man and I respect him. We have never had a great deal to say to each other, although he and my mother have mutual discussions that never end. Anyway, he is my father, and this man Bailey is not.) I said again that I was keeping him from his work, wasn't I?

He said no, and sat there waiting for me.

I stopped trying to be impressive, and I began to talk very fast, not preparing my words at all. I said that I thought Mig might be mixed up in pushing drugs, and that he was certainly mixed up with some girl whose name was not Anna. I said I suppose it was to be expected of him but that I was fed to the teeth with his sliding and cheating and conniving. I then said that I thought I was beginning to hate Mig.

All he said was, "You mustn't." One more degree of temperature and I would surely boil, but at the moment I was seething just enough to give me a sense of exquisite irresponsibility. I said, "Why shouldn't I hate him, if I may presume to ask?" and then, before he could answer, I flapped a hand to hush him and said dismissively, "I know. Don't tell me. It's unchristian."

He said he had not planned to tell me so. My temperature rose the fatal degree, and I gave the short, competent bark of a laugh that I save for emergencies. I said unpleasantly, "My remark didn't give satisfaction, did it?"

He said, astounding me, that I was being rude.

I could not get up and walk away from him, and I could not just sit there like a child reproved for not washing its hands before coming to the dinner table. My body shuffled. I could feel it shuffling, the whole of it; there was not a bone I knew what to do with it. I did the classical thing and looked at my feet, almost feeling them jerk with wanting to escape. My shoes held them fast.

I gathered my noble rags around me and said, with as much ice as I could summon (I who had been boiling so very recently), that I was sorry if I had seemed rude but that I had a right to hate Mig. I thought to myself in a very dignified manner that this Christian father was pushing me over the very boundary that he disapproved. I would hate Mig now, if only to show my independence. My feet stopped trying to shuffle.

Father Bailey said, "When did you decide?" and I thought my mind had played a trick on me and I had missed something he had said.

"Decide what?" I felt stupid again, and I thought resentfully that he probably wanted me to feel stupid.

"To start hating Mig."

I looked at my hands for a change of scenery. Eight fingers, two thumbs, bony, a white scar across the back of right-hand knuckles where I had warded off a razor-sharp knife in my early days on the street before I learned never to argue. I thought the knife's slash gave me some authority. I could hate anyone I wanted to—except that Father Bailey wasn't asking about my hating Mig but about my deciding to hate him. Phrased that way, it had a certain cold-blooded lack of charm,

I lost my upright posture, and I put my hands away where I could not see the white knuckle-cut.

"I should have said that I *will* hate Mig," I said carefully, "when he deserves it."

"And if he doesn't?"

"He will." I was confident enough to look at him then, but he was not looking at me and so my self-confidence went unnoticed. Even now, I don't know whether he was being inattentive or clever.

He rocked himself a little on his unrocking chair, tipping backwards and reminding me of my Uncle Edward. My Uncle Edward visits his sister, my mother, at regular unannounced intervals. He is a political reactionary, and he always rocks his chair just before he damns whatever generation or statesman is most in the news. My mother says "Now, Edward!", my father has sold him a fat insurance policy, and I either avoid him altogether or spring into anarchy on contact. He never listens to me. He never even tells me that I am being rude, which, to him, I quite often am but so skillfully that he can't quite prove it.

Watching Father Bailey rock like my Uncle Edward, I came suddenly into beautiful balance. My hands were no longer too large and too bony, my feet did not shuffle. I waited to hear what the good Father Bailey might have to say.

The front legs of his chair came down, and he looked at me for a minute. "In other words," he said in a curiously orderly way, "you assume that the evil in Mig will automatically overcome the good."

I accepted his packaged thought as offered and turned it over inside my head. I then said that, in a lousy street, in a lousy country, in a lousy world, what else did he expect me to assume? He had me talking back at him just the way I talk back to Uncle Edward, and I wanted my words unsaid as soon as they came out. On the other hand, I was curious to see how he would answer them. (This is a curse on me. I once told Professor Blount that I found Chekhov very limited in concept. He said pleasantly, "Yes, I expect you do," and I rolled myself up in the doormat and crept away.)

Father Bailey, however, simply said that it wasn't a lousy street at all. Just enough of the truth was on his side. "Okay, a lousy street full of good people," I conceded. "But I don't think I trust Mig."

"I wasn't really talking about Mig."

"I don't think I trust anybody. I don't even trust myself."

"I wasn't talking about you either."

I spotted my layman's advantage and leaned back in my chair, feeling very much in control. Indeed, I knew this sermon-vendor of old. "Ah," I said sardonically, "you mean Something Bigger than Myself?"

There was a pause, and then he said, rather too gently, "You don't feel that there *is* anything bigger than yourself?"

I left very soon after that, having nothing much more to say.

He has caught me, fairly enough, on my blind side, the side of my apprehension and my loneliness. I have drifted, stumbled, lurched and battled on this street of mine, and my bright brave whistle gets fainter by the minute. I am more frightened every day, not frightened of anything that the street can do to me but frightened of finding that it all adds up to nothing, and that no one—not the social workers and not the clergy, not the students, the anarchists and the politicians, not the scientists, the drug pushers, the homemakers, the teachers, the storekeepers, not the fat cats and not the hungry dogs—*no one* is doing anything more than to hang on perilously, head above water, smiling or screaming according to their will and their wont, and always talking endlessly. Talking, and talking, and talking.

Goddammit! I want something more!!

Be calm, Richard, be calm. The Foundation would not like to hear your typewriter screaming that way. If you cannot be calm in the night's small dark hours, when *can* you be calm? Not in the morning; the street is too full, too soon, of too much. Not at noon; noon here is very high. Not at twilight, when all the cats are gray. And apparently not even late at night, as now, when it is unseasonably cold and there have been no recent screams outside the window and only a few curses, and the rats nibble-nibble in someone's walls somewhere, but, happily, not in mine. Just a world, tick-tocking itself into eternity.

Certainly I believe there is something bigger than myself. The question is, does It know that I am here?

18

By now, Anna knew that the trap had closed. The baby was, most certainly, not dead inside her.

She thought dimly of killing herself, but like Mig she was afraid of death. She thought sickly of Mama Kraus and turned her mind sickly away from the thought. She thought of Father Bailey and of Mrs. Detty, of Mr. Harris who had been kind to Mig, and of the other people in the street, but none of them could help her if Jesus couldn't.

And she prayed to Jesus with terrible sincerity. She—who had wanted a kitten of her own since childhood, who ached for every lame pigeon, every hungry sparrow—now prayed, through all her waking hours, for a baby's death. Her face thinned and her eyes grew, and she huddled in a shawl to deny the thickening of her body. She knew she was getting close to that unendurable moment when Mig would know that she had lied to him, telling him that everything was all right.

Then he would throw her out, and it would not matter any longer what became of her. She could not conceive of a world without him. When he had told her that night that she was to go back to her family, a brief flower of intense joy had bloomed inside her. And when she had found that he meant her to go alone, she had wanted to die. As she wished now that the baby would die.

Would it, really, be so terrible to go once more to Mama Kraus? Could it be more terrible than to lose Mig?

At the back of Anna's aching mind, there persisted the conviction that, if only she had a little book knowledge, she could get help. Sometimes she would take out her copy of the women's magazine, Mig's gift, and leaf through its bright, glazed pages, looking for an answer. There were a few easy words that she could understand, but then they linked to others that were empty of meaning because she was empty of knowledge. She would have looked for an answer on television, but she had promised Mig never to turn the set on unless he was there (it would explode? she would learn something he did not want her to know? there was some law?) and she really did not understand most of the shows he watched, although she laughed eagerly whenever he did and was grave when he was grave.

No, she did not know anything, and so there was no escape. At least, Mama Kraus had promised to do it—whatever it was— without asking for her money right away. She called Anna "my little bird" and said she would wait to be paid. She was kind, she was really very kind . . . . . Anna clasped her hands over the cross that Mig had given her, so tightly that it bit her palms, and she thought with terrified eyes of how very kind Mama Kraus was.

Each morning she weighed in her mind the fear of Mama Kraus against the fear of losing Mig, and each morning the scales tipped more plainly. In the end, she knew that there was really no choice, and the argument in her head stopped.

From that moment of clear decision, Anna walked more easily and became once more aware of sunshine and of people's faces. The greedy fullness inside her gave way to a kind of contentment, and everything seemed very simple. When she knew she could no longer hide the baby from Mig, she would go straight to Mama Kraus. Until that moment, she need not think about it at all. So she walked straight and felt better than she had for a long time and was more in love with Mig than she could believe.

As for him, he grew more young cock than ever, extending his influence and his little empire. Since he had no idea that Anna's revival reflected a peace of mind that came from having made a choice and a peace of body that came from being over the early stages of her pregnancy, he was able to rejoice in it and in a revival of his own. He had been grainy, unsure, running to Mr. Harris, shaking whenever he saw a cop. Now, he noticed the sun and he noticed his neighbors. He noticed, also, that those men who let him have the room for no price but his silence now chose to come less often but to stay longer. They told him ahead of time when to get out, and he went, taking Anna with him. He even took her to the park once, but she got tired too soon because she was lazy from being home all day, so he took her to a movie in a cheap house. Since it was all in Spanish, neither of them could make anything of it but he found it absorbing because the men in it moved with such ruthless splendor. He sometimes thought he might be partly Spanish himself, not Puerto Rican because he was superior to foreigners, but Spanish, although at the back of his mind he was painfully aware that he was not anything at all. Not anything now. Later.

Thinking of later, he began to study the men who gave him his room. He memorized their faces and their voices and the hours they kept and which direction they walked in when they reached the street. He stored it all away.

One night, he had seen Mr. Harris bring a girl home with him, and then he had taken the trouble to see that the girl did not leave until just before dawn, and he stored that away too. Mr. Harris would probably not care who knew what he did, not up here. But down there where Mr. Harris's Foundation was, somebody might care enough to make it a thing worth

103

knowing. He, Mig, would never tell them, of course, but if Mr. Harris knew that he knew, he might—he might—

A dream spun itself out in Mig's mind, a golden dream as ruthless as murder but, unlike murder, exquisitely detached. He fondled power in his mind, counting a rosary of what he knew about Ernie and Ernie's friends, Mr. Harris and Mr. Harris's girl, the men who used the room in the security of its eyelessness. He felt marvelously strong, silky-fingered, free even from the street's day and night boredom, lord of the castle and clever as sin.

19

I thought that Mrs. Detty knew everything. I thought that any piece of advice she gave me would be hammered out of pure, mysterious gold and that all I needed to do was to rub her like a magician's lamp. I sought her out, I suspect, from loneliness. I know that I sighed loudly enough so that she would be sure to hear me.

"You need a change," she said. "You don't even go to the movies." Comforted by being the object of her expansive, worldwide, interplanetary solicitude, I asked her why she thought I needed a change. Did the creases in my brow and my pants belie my merry spirit? did grim night peep from my damask cheek?

She said I looked sallow, deflating me. It happens that her skin is somewhat leathered and close to coal black, while mine is what is inaccurately known to us propped-up whites as flesh-colored. It does not become Mrs. Detty to throw my color in my face. I was born sallow and have remained so, although my mother fed me on liver and soybeans at an early age and my father exercised me on the end of a beach ball. My grandfather was as red as a rose, and it seems to me that any child of spirit, coming from such a wholesome family, could not help being pasty. I told Mrs. Detty this, elaborating on my theme, and she kept right on spindling limp papers on a spindle which belongs to an obliging Sicilian grocer whose back room she sometimes uses as her office. I have often wondered if she bills the city for office rent, and I am not going to inquire into the matter because, whatever she may double-deal from the city, she undoubtedly plows back into her clients' pockets.

Mrs. Detty's method of spindling is ruthless, like a shrike's. She writes all her memos with a green ballpoint pen. She keeps copies of nothing. She once killed a rat in a baby's crib, with the heel of her shoe, and she cried afterwards because the baby didn't. When she told me about it, I offered to wrap up a dead rat in brown paper and send it to our councilman through the mails. She wouldn't let me do it because she said he was a good man and, months later, when I had to see him about an evicted family, I found out that she was perfectly right. I was very shook up about this because I had learned at my mother's knee that all politicians are crooks, which proves that you can't trust anything, not even a mother's knee.

Mrs. Detty shriked a last piece of paper and told me again that I needed a change. I said that Lonergan-Logan was about to win an all-expense jet flight to the Indies and had promised to take me with him, since the prize contest is structured for a honeymoon couple. (It would be just like him to make good on this one; I see us lolling on the beach, our coconut-palm hats in eternal tandem, bound by my pledge to share his fortunes.)

Mrs. Detty read my mind and said not to worry, that Mr. Logan (which is what she calls him, being more decisive than I am) would not win. I asked her what she did herself when she needed a change, and she said that she went out and looked for a different place to live. I asked her if she needed one, because if she did I was prepared to force some landlord at knife-point to give it to her, but she said no. She said hunting for another apartment was just in the line of business; if she could find a place adequate for one person, she could then fit a family of six into it. She made this observation without any ill will, and she added, "I don't want to move, anyway. The mirror in my bathroom is the only mirror I ever had that makes me look the way I'd like to look."

I said "Maybe it's the light?" and she said no, it was a hundred-watt bulb, and I realized I had said something rude without meaning to but that she was not insulted. I felt so comfortable sitting there in her corner of the world that everything suddenly seemed very simple and I heard myself asking, quite placidly, if she knew Jeannie's telephone number.

She shook her head. "Just the old one, but maybe she never moved."

I knew powerfully at that moment that Jeannie not only had not moved but that she would answer the telephone at once and that she would remember me as I remembered her phone number. I felt in my pocket and found a dime and I told Mrs. Detty that I had remembered something I was supposed to do. She was making green scratches in a notebook by that time, and, when I left, she did not notice me and I did not care. I was sallow and I needed a change. She had told me everything I needed to know.

Mind you, this was while I still believed that Mrs. Detty was running the world.

I tried to call Jeannie from a phone booth. The phone was, of course, out of order and it breathed silence like a seashell. I stood holding the receiver to my ear, staring at the garbage that had found its way into the booth and feeling all my loneliness come back, a stealthy cat loneliness, waiting for me when no one was there to hold my hand. I left the telephone dangling and breathing, and I set out fiercely to hunt for another, repeating the digits of Jeannie's number out loud as if they were a charm.

The next phone booth was gutted, stripped, the coin box violated. And the next and the next. I followed some sick passionate stranger from booth to booth, some groping mad-man desperate for a fix and without the price of a stick of chewing gum to buy it with. Or perhaps, by now, he had it, and his pockets were glutted with corporation dimes, his body breathing seashell silence, and his spirit was in hell.

What would Father Bailey say to that use of the word "spirit," I wondered, and I felt the same resentment I had before. I told myself that if I reached Jeannie I would not know what to ask her, did not even know why I had wanted to call. (Oh yes, I knew.) And when I found, over the hills and far away, rhyming nursery-sweet for my need, a working telephone, I was suddenly afraid to dial her number. I stood there numbly with the instrument in my hand, listening not to a seashell of nothing but to the efficient purr of a mechanical device.

After an eternity, I dialled the seven digits, one by one with exquisite precision. The last spun off my finger, and the phone, Jeannie's phone, began to ring. It rang and rang and rang. I stood there hearing it and completely incapable of believing that she was not going to answer, until some kind of thin sanity came back to me and I realized she would be at work. I must call her in the evening. I must call her from my own telephone, not from this ship's cabin on a street, with beer cans and newspapers and scatological delicacies lapping at my feet. For God's sake, I thought, if they would just clean the sidewalks, just once, just use clean water on the open sores of the gutters and bind up the coin boxes—And even the water is polluted and the money is polluted, I thought, and I hit the black tele-phone box with my fist and I yelled to Jeannie to answer me. Goddammit, answer me!

And then I walked out of there as cool and quiet as if I had found my own particular fix, and I put Jeannie into a back corner of my mind and went about the rest of my day as if I had never gone mad at all.

I called her at six o'clock that night, from my own room, feeling confident and secure and knowing what I would say. There was no answer. I called her again at seven, at eight, at nine, at ten. Finally, in despair, I called her at midnight. By then, frustration had linked with desire, and I was literally sick. I thought of all the ways open to me of finding relief, and then I stumbled across the room, fell onto my bed and, stone-blind, stone-deaf and stone-cold, I slept.

I was wakened in broad daylight by the telephone ringing, and my heart knew who was calling me and it lurched. When I answered, it was a woman's voice all right, but she wanted a hospital, not me. I told her to take me to the hospital with her, and she hung up and probably went and washed her hands with strong soap. I thought how terribly easy it is to turn mean, and then I got dressed and ate a large breakfast and, sober and healthy, I wrote three reports for the Foundation, all of them composed in the half-light of truth and lie and all designed to promote the good life as I saw it.

My first news of the street was that we had had another homicide during the night, a lover's quarrel between two males and only one of them left alive. There was a small reporter hanging around, still taking notes—a very small reporter, indicating the pettiness of our local scene. I had known the dead man and rather liked him, and I was coolly aware that anything I said to the Press would be misconstrued, so I kept my mouth shut like a respectable coward. The person who stayed on to talk with him was Father Bailey, who has chosen his own way of life and who is presumably immune to such hazards.

Mrs. Detty would have stayed, I suppose. God knows, Mrs. Detty did not choose her way of life and she is not immune to anything. The step forward is that I can call myself a coward without cringing. Or is that a step backward, perhaps?

I am making too much of the whole thing. It is not me who is dead in a street murder, but another man who was born into the wrong culture, in the wrong place, at the wrong time. Good morning, Father-Bailey-my-giant, isn't it a great world as you were telling me?

I turned so rock-cold that I got three times my usual work done. When I got home, my telephone was ringing and my heart did nothing unusual at all. I knew that the voice at the other end would not be Jeannie's.

As, of course, it was not. It was Codd's, bright and hearty. He was throwing another party, could I come, would I like to come? I said "Sure," doing him a big favor.

Bring a girl, he said, bring a harem. I heard myself saying—absolutely casual (I would have flicked the ash off my cigarette if I had been smoking) —thanks no, I'd have one of his. The remark went over very big. He guffawed, and he probably slapped his knee. If I had been within his reach, he would have punched me jovially in the ribs. I saw his gigantic wink project itself on the ceiling over my head.

See, Jeannie, see? I thought savagely. See Richard jump? See Richard play?

I heard the noise that is like no other noise on earth even before I got off the elevator in Codd's mink-walled apartment building—every voice in pursuit of itself, every ear turned inward, every eye looking for its own face in the cocktail glass, in the chance mirror, in the contesting eyeball. I took the first drink that went past me on a tray, and I took it medicinally, being assailed by the mimic violence of cocktail voices and the mimic show of self-exploiting talk. Having made this Olympian judgment, I felt someone touch my elbow and I turned to find Codd, the good host, making me welcome. I responded with such fervor that it was painfully clear that my need to feel superior had come from my conviction that I was not really wanted.

Codd said, "Greetings, brother" from a terribly old joke we

had shared in our college days, and I said, "Greetings, brother" and understood, so late in the day, all that the academic world had done for me. (My family paid for those four years, I didn't.) "Want-you-to-meet," he said and, seizing my elbow, he began to pilot me around, introducing me to faces, to bodies, to beards, pipes, skirts, eyelashes, presenting me in each encounter as if I were his distinguished son home for the holidays.

"Fresh from the ghetto," he said proudly, thrusting me at a young man in a blue shirt and no jacket and a beard so untidy that it must have been trimmed that way. We bowed formally, and I kept my sword-arm free. He had a girl on his, a small one in an unbecoming tan dress, dark soft bangs and too much eye makeup. Her face was tiny and fierce, rather like a young squirrel's. "Do you teach?" she said, and I answered helplessly, unable to stop myself, that I wrote novels.

The bearded pard raised a hairy eyebrow, and his beard stirred. He said, "So do I. Who's your publisher?"

I had nowhere to go. I said insolently, "Who's yours?" and he told me. At that point I recognized his name, which Codd had only mumbled, and I remembered the title of his novel and even a line from a review in the Times, which had said that the young author "challenged the assumptions of our age." How pompous, I had thought, and how I would have loved to hear it said about some novel of mine!

Now I punished myself. I said that I had written only one novel and that it had not yet been accepted. I was rewriting it, I said, I had a new concept. I think I may have used the word "viable." A tray passed me, tinkling, and I reached emotionally for salvation.

The squirrel-face said that I must get a lot of inspiration working in a ghetto, and oddly enough my bearded enemy nodded respectfully. "You work for the City?"

We were off the fiction hook, and I breathed more freely.

111

I said I worked for a foundation, and she murmured at me "Great! Really great!" and then someone very blonde stepped in and took her escort away from her and left us standing alone.

Codd went by, smiled knowingly and said "I see you found one," and I felt two-drinks-in and a child of my time. This girl was wearing too much eye makeup, but she was mine and I hoped Jeannie was watching from somewhere. After that, everything moved too fast. The trays were attentive and I referred to them pretty conscientiously, and the squirrel-child (whose name turned out to be Ellyn with a *y*) became attentive too and was my credential with each new knot of guests as we circled the room. Someone told me, at a moment when I had briefly mislaid her, that her father was very rich and that she was looking for a ghetto to use as a playpen, but this turned out to be not completely true. She had got herself a degree in Psychology and was now working in a public relations office. Along about the time that she had made it quite clear that her boss would not fire her, and why, I was beginning to notice that her teeth were a little pointed. But she clung to me, and I clung to her.

So I took her home, and why not? She wanted a ghetto and a thrill, and I wanted to revenge myself on Jeannie for not being home when her telephone rang, and on the already-published young man with a beard, and on Codd for having so much money, and on my street for being so foul and pathetic and vicious and abandoned.

I don't know what it was that she wanted to revenge herself on. Something. We gave each other a hard night. I woke in a sick dawn to find that she had left me, and I was hollow with dread all day, expecting to hear street rumors ("Lone Girl Found Stabbed") until I remembered the name of the man she worked for and I called his office and asked for her with the *y* in Ellyn clearly pronounced.

When she answered, I hung up. It really was, all of it, Shakespeare's expense of spirit in a waste of shame, since what I was trying to do was to get the attention of someone, out there, wanting (in defiance of Codd's hospitality) only to offend, not to wound.

My therapeutic jaunt into that brave foreign world has done me no good. The street has closed around me more tightly than ever.

20

What Mig had been afraid of finally happened. Ernie got caught.

A plan had been made for a productive descent on a nice store in a nice neighborhood, where the owner was occasionally careless about taking defensive measures. Ernie had brooded on this and had then hatched his arrangements with real artistry, promising Mig beautiful dividends and a foretaste of glory. The very elegance of the undertaking went to Ernie's head, and he celebrated his own genius by getting a hard high. ("I tell you, Mig, it don't do nothing to me, just makes me sharper. I cut it to nothing, Mig, way down to a little toehold.") It had not been cut and it did not make him sharper, only gigantic in his skull and omnipotent in his body, so that he thought he could do anything. Greater than Caesar, he spun down the street, hours ahead of his obedient-monkey command, intending only to look things over.

In his brain, the pattern was beautiful, as clear as the stars that leaned over him, but his feet were fools and his hands betrayed him like twin harlots. He imagined himself to be a moving shadow; he believed that his body flowed in the darkness.

His body did not flow; it jerked. Every move he made clanged, and even his bones were psychedelic. A passing patrolman, operating on a schedule that did not slide and rot like the one in Ernie's cooked brain, stopped to watch him. When Ernie—celestial, invisible, in winged flight—leaned from Heaven to examine the lock on the storefront door, the hand of the Law came down on his shoulder.

The cop was a Negro, and, although Ernie was certainly nothing so traditional as a racist, he lived in a white skin on a street where the majority was black and he had a working man's distrust of superior numbers. His snowy airborne haze was split by black shock, and he did an extraordinary thing. He bit the cop on the wrist, screaming the small obscenities of a Victorian fishwife. The cop dropped him like a wasp, then scooped him up again, and they stared at each other briefly in open, uncivilized hatred.

But the cop was thirty-five and operating in his own area, while Ernie was sixteen and out of his. The brief moment of glory (teeth sunk in human flesh) faded. The cop did not hit him, and Ernie did not bite again.

He cried all the way to the station house, out of sheer frustration and fright, and, having foolishly lied about his age, he spent a night in jail. The uniform that turned a key on him remarked unfeelingly that, if the victim got rabies, the prisoner would get the electric chair. Ernie was not as distressed by this as he should have been; he knew enough about dogs to know that he was not one. Toward morning he slept fairly well, though foggily, and he woke without headache or hallucination.

It was Father Bailey who got him out, word having reached him through the inevitable street channels. Ernie had an eleven-year-old camp follower named Lou, who loved him silently because he left her alone, which no one else did. When she heard of her beloved's disaster, she went straight to Mig, tears streaming from her eyes and her long rusty-black hair in a gypsy's tangle. Mig, cold with fury and contempt, sent her to Father Bailey, believing that any church, however small, must have influence. For himself, he would gladly have left Ernie behind walls forever, but an instinct for self-preservation warned him where the trail would lead if Ernie chose to talk.

Father Bailey offered Lou no comfort, since that was not what she wanted, but he took the necessary steps. Ernie, inexplicably a first offender, was duly handed over; the clergyman looked at him for a long time, said almost nothing, and sent him on his way. Ernie, who had been thinking in terms of repentance and salvation and was eager for both, felt deprived, and when he departed, the cold lump just behind his belt buckle was occasioned less by Christian remorse than by simple dread of facing Mig.

In this, he was fully justified. Coldly, mercilessly, explicitly, Mig saw to it that he was humiliated, in his own eyes and in the eyes of his followers. This was necessary, since, if Ernie retained any self-respect or pardon, he would become worse than useless. He was even forbidden to speak to Anna.

So, for her, one more little tendril of trust and affection was broken off. There had been a kind of jauntiness about Ernie that had made her believe it was possible for someone to enjoy the world. She had liked this, as a possibility and as a hope.

The brief summer of her own hope was closing, and she knew that she could not hide the future much longer from Mig. She would have to go to Mama Kraus, but she put it off from day to day, hoping she would die before it happened. In the meantime, in the cold void, she missed Ernie. Like the cross and the television set and the magazine, he had been something to hold onto.

21

Mig's squirmy little friend and bellhop, whose name is Ernie, got himself in trouble last night. He bit a cop—a black cop, at that. When I was much younger, say, a couple of months ago, I would have been stirred by this show of independence and galloped to the sinner's rescue. Now I walk the streets in my old-man mood, and I shrug my shoulders, and I let Father Bailey take the responsibility. After all, the cultivation and defense of cop-chewers is not the kind of civil action that my Father Foundation would approve, so I have both reason and self-interest on my side.

Or, to put it less generously, I copped out. I did not choose to rescue Ernie, because I did not want to have him leaning on me the way Mig leans on me. I no longer want to play God. I no longer want the responsibility which is the only reason I ever came to these Dark-Age medieval streets in the first place. I came to educate, to elevate, to improve, did I not? And, of course, to write.

I think I am a thousand years old. Too old even to take any cynical pleasure in my own schoolboy anguish. I sit at this type-writer as if I were sitting in a boat, trailing my hand in the water, wishing the world would go away, putting off the future.

Ernie, linked as he is to Mig, was *my* job, not Father Bailey's, but my indifference is total. The frost line inside me is so deep tonight that I am no longer even sorry for myself. I would like to know what I am doing here (not on this street, which I chose, but on this globe, this planet, this eye in space), but I suppose everyone would like to know that. I can see them all pondering the question. Mrs. Detty of a Thursday morning, putting her hat on before that mirror which befriends her image: "Good morning, dear, what are you doing on this giddy earth?" Lonergan-Logan, clipping a new hope out of an ad that glows with benevolent promise: "What is it all about? Does God's Plan include my going to the Bahamas?" Pollo, who has lately been whirled off the planet altogether and may or may not be beyond such conjectures. Codd, waking at dawn with a blonde and no headache, the blonde chanting her metaphysical "What-am-I-doing-here-darling?" and Codd magnificently misunderstanding her message and responding inappropriately. My black giantess. My black Cassy and my white Irmalee. Jeannie, who is only waiting for me to phone though she is never there— "What am I doing by the phone," Jeannie asks herself, "waiting for my own true love, who is no longer really quite certain, so much later, what my face looks like?" Anna, lost kitten. Mig, strange cat. Father Bailey . . . . .

Aha. Father Bailey. *He,* at least, knows what he is doing here. Father Bailey has sought, and he has found. He has knocked, and the door has been opened unto him. Father Bailey is an enlightened man, an energetic pilgrim, a member of the Elect, a fount of knowledge, the one true vessel.

I am indeed happy to surrender the responsibility of Ernie to the good Father. He is the man for the job.

But how did he know that I wouldn't do it? Why didn't he even call me? *Why did he have to be right?*

Well, as usual, the typewriter has drawn my poison. Perhaps Ernie's first sweet taste of a public servant has drawn his. We can meet understandingly, and I will be to Ernie all the nice brotherly things I meant to be to Mig, who has changed his yielding character and now makes me feel that I am being exploited. Ernie, on the other hand, is full of endearing virtues. He is kind to cockroaches, generous to stringy cats and stray dogs; he dips babies into milkcans where they can sup their fill, punctures a black-cop thumb with his white-civilian teeth in sheer high spirits, so young is Ernie, so brilliantly stupid, so led by the nose and by Mig's hands. Perhaps Ernie would be a bulwark against Mig's invasion of me. Perhaps Father Bailey will give Ernie to me as a present. I can do penance on his baby brows, tie a silken cord around the new lamb's neck . . . . .

Feed on another life? Is *that* my trouble?

Never mind. I am washed clean. I can now go to Father Bailey and tell him manfully that I will take over Ernie and I will guarantee to build him up skillfully, blob by blob. My own tired feet of clay will reassure Ernie that he is not alone. I will put the lad into a vocational school and he will learn a trade, learn the fine brave use of his own fine brave hands. He will grow up and marry Cassy or Irmalee, or both if he cannot choose between them. And that, my darling Jeannie, (and it is true that I no longer know whether your hair was brown or yellow) is why I was put into this world, to take Ernie's little grimy paw and lead him into fresh fields and pastures new. Exit, rejoicing.

This is very fine. I might have been a novelist, had I but recognized my talent at an early age. Professor Blount recognized it, but he died of green-sickness and too many seminars. That brave bastard at Codd's party wrote a novel and got it published, but Ellyn came to *my* bed, borne on my shield.——— Well, no, I won't pursue that. The fair Ellyn must have shared his bed o' nights rather better than she shared mine.

It is eleven o'clock. I could get the late news report on my little black transistor radio, or I could telephone Jeannie one more time on my little black telephone.

It is eleven-fifteen, and I have missed the late news. Jeannie is not in. She must be dead, like Professor Blount. It is quite true that I can scarcely remember what she looks like. She is only a sweet meadow inside my head, and I cling to her because I would like to believe in something good.

But I really do not believe that anything is good, and I suppose that is my first little death. I shall be all the better for it, no doubt, once I get over the peculiar and somewhat awful sensation of being perfectly hollow.

Richard Harris fit the Battle of Jericho, and the walls have come tumbling down. There remains a small neat knapsack in the middle of a green plain, and a voice is saying "Duty to my Foundation, to my Country, and to my God." In that order.

Someone has been polluting my beer. I never wrote so well.

22

Lying on the bed with Anna beside him, he had been watching television for the past two hours, and his head swam with a confusion of images like the specks that gather before a sun-watcher's eyes. Now he looked without seeing, and his mind sorted in exasperation among a dozen plans, each one designed to make that fortune that waited him forever just beyond the next corner.

He was beginning to regret having crushed Ernie, turning him into something as useless as a dead insect. If Ernie was around, he could at least be sent out to dig up another TV set, this time in color. The jerky, distant, black-and-white blondes would become ravishing and real, their skin exciting, their hues so tender that hands could almost touch.

He stared bleakly at the fraudulent screen, some lonely corner of his bored brain telling him that even a rainbow of blondes on it would not satisfy him. The picture on the screen jumped in its frame. The voice went on talking, crisp, urgent, delivering its soap message, housewife, child, dirty dress, clean dress, happiness-soiled, happiness-cleaned. The frames began to jump wildly like a pack of cards being shuffled, and the housewife split into serene halves, her shoes above her hair.

Mig sighed, yawned and stretched, young animal. Anna's

hand fell away from his, it must have been lying there for a long time. He felt the destructive power that comes from holding someone else's lifeline, and he said "Anna" carelessly to hear her murmur his name in answer and nestle closer. She did so exactly, and he was promptly disappointed, wishing her to hurl herself against him, to encompass him, to drown him in passion.

He sighed again, exquisitely bored and no nearer fortune than usual. His six-handed semi-landlord had not been around for almost two weeks, and a worry nagged at the back of Mig's brain. Curious things happened to sallow, red-eyed men who met each other in empty rooms with paper packets. Sometimes the earth swallowed them up; sometimes, jails. They vanished and returned and vanished again like a vague choking smoke.

Suppose, however, that this time they didn't come back at all? Suppose someone else came to take possession of these four walls?

"Anna?"

She stirred.

"You seen the men lately?"

She knew who the men were. She shook her head against his shoulder.

He thought hard for a full minute, wondering who owned this half-gutted building anyway, whether he could find out, and, if so, whether he could learn something very, very clever that would give him the hold he needed. (Give him a hold on the world, and he could pull it up by its rivers and swing it around his head.) "Maybe they've gone away," he said.

He said just the four words, and she knew exactly what he was thinking. She pressed against him softly and answered him in her soft, small voice. He was not to worry, they could pay rent somehow if they had to, she would go out and get a job. He said, "You? Where?" scornfully, because she knew nothing about life at all.

In a store, she told him.

He started to laugh at her, and then he started to think again. After a moment, he sat up on the side of the bed and looked at the good alligator shoes that had been so conveniently supplied to fill his needs. The good alligator shoes had been very easy to come by.

In its corner, the TV set went on talking, yearning, commanding, coaxing, displaying its peacock ads, wheedling its commercials, leering its expensive dreams. Mig went over and turned it off, and then he came back to Anna and studied her with a new kind of interest. It was quite possible that she could get a job clerking in a store, and if so she could become very useful—useful as Ernie had been useful. She looked as honest as an angel. She could learn to be light-fingered.

He picked her hand up and examined the narrow wrist, thin enough to break but very quick, very supple. Anna could take Ernie's place in time. And he, Mig, would continue as before. Untouchable.

He put Anna's hand down, then leaned over and took her face between his palms. Thin, pale, eyes enormous. His heart misgave him. Who would hire her? Who would want her? His pinwheel plan stopped spinning and fell apart. His plans often did.

What Anna needed was milk. Milk was what all scrawny people needed, like the scrawny street cats who had never tasted milk. Mig had countless medical theories about life, and milk was one of them. People on Welfare got it for the asking, in vast quantities. It splashed on their doorsteps, fattened their bellies, nourished them like rain on weeds.

He freed her little pinched face from his hands and said aloud, as an article of faith, "You need milk." It came to him triumphantly, as soon as he had said it, that all he need do was to go to Richard Harris and ask for money for Anna's health. Kind Mr. Harris, good Mr. Harris, was so very fond of Anna, so *very* fond . . . . .

For a second, Mig's mind leaped beyond Anna as store clerk

to Anna as something else, far more profitable and far easier to arrange. He rejected the idea as quickly as it came, not only because it touched the vein of his own possessiveness but because it also touched something else in him that was more confusing.

No matter. He did not need any other plans for Anna. Not while he had Mr. Harris, and Mr. Harris had his Foundation.

23

I suppose what I really wanted was to go to confession. I wanted to proclaim my sins and to be absolved. I dressed for the event very carefully. I polished my chain mail, burnished my lance and rode my great charger into Father Bailey's rooms. There I announced grandly that I was prepared to assume all responsibility for Ernie. Father Bailey said, No.

My jaw dropped, endangering my plumed helmet. My armor and my spine sagged. My palfrey galloped away. Or, not to be so fancy about it all, I sat and stared like a moron, mouth open for catching flies. After a moment, I rallied and decided that I had misunderstood him or that, more likely, he had misunderstood me. I began once more to explain and, if I say so myself, I explained very nicely.

I really was trying to be nice, and I was trying to be honorable. I knew perfectly well that I had run out on Ernie, and I wanted to make up for it and start over again. I did not want a frail old clergyman assuming my responsibilities, doing my job. I yearned for virtue, for the dawn of a new era. And all he said was, No.

As on other occasions with Father Bailey, I felt my temperature soaring. This time I was not being rebuked; I was being thwarted. I had come to him with clean paws and a willing heart, only to be sent back into my corner, me with my Boy

Scout hatchet at the ready and no motivation except to help an old gentleman across a difficult street.

I said "Very well" icily, and I got to my feet. He waved me down and said, very gently and very rudely, "Why do you want Ernie?"

My hackles rose. I said stiffly that I did not *want* Ernie. I said that I merely felt a certain obligation toward him and that I had failed in my duty. I really said that about duty, and I never even winced. In the background, my Foundation must have squared its shoulders and thrown out its chest, proud of this fine lad of theirs who is not afraid to use such four-letter words, long since in disrepute. Obviously, I made no impression on Father Bailey. Duty is his doxy.

He said merely, "Is it because Ernie is a friend of your Mig?"

I said he was not *my* Mig, showing an increased dependence on italics.

"You don't feel responsible for him?"

I replied sullenly that being responsible was not the same thing as being possessive, which cheered me for a moment because it seemed to be a rather agile retort. Father Bailey had not, however, been talking about possessiveness, and I knew it. As usual, his indefatigable silence wore me down and, after a little honest thinking (a luxury I must learn not to permit myself) I admitted that, yes, I did feel responsible for Mig. I then added, without really meaning to, "I'm not sure it's done Mig much good. Perhaps that's why I dodged Ernie." The moment I had blurted out that quite unnecessary admission, I felt suddenly ten years old. I was back in my own yard, explaining to my father why I caught balls so badly when he threw them to me, out behind our garage, just on twilight, after he got home from work. Always so earnest about me, my father was. Very kind, very conscientious. I looked at this new and much odder father, sitting opposite me now, and I thought that what I really wanted was someone who would just trust me to do my best, which he wasn't doing. He was letting me down. Like Jeannie, who had gone away. Like Mrs. Detty who was too busy, Ellyn who quit me, Codd who lived on another planet——Daddy! HELP! Dear God Almighty, please throw me a ball that I can catch!

If I have a weakness (I have), it is that I tend to be unduly pleased when I produce this kind of philosophical metaphor. It gratified me, and I smiled to myself—satirically, no doubt, true to my profession.

Father Bailey said "Joke?" mildly.

After all, what did it matter who took the responsibility for Ernie, so long as someone did? I leaned back and crossed my legs like a literary man. "A passing blasphemous thought," I said lightly. "At least, I suppose it was blasphemous. I won't offend you with it." I thought that last touch was distinctly elegant.

Father Bailey began to hunt for his pipe. He has only one, and he keeps it in the middle of his table under whatever pile of papers is in the ascendancy. I have never seen him light it, but he spends a lot of time hunting. It appeared this time to be more elusive than usual, and it also appeared that he had taken a vow of silence until it was found. My mind began to twitch. I uncrossed my legs and sat up, compulsively chatty as usual. "Still," said I, the brightest man in Philosophy III, "one man's blasphemy is another man's theology."

He found the pipe. He turned it over and knocked it out, and he missed the ashtray by a matter of miles. He then put the pipe down carefully, brushed the mess he had made onto a piece of paper which had some figures scribbled on it, put everything into the ashtray and began to look around for something else—presumably his tobacco. I found it for him in plain sight (is the whole thing a put-on?) and he thanked me and laid it down on top of a bound copy of the National Geographic, which I happen to know was given to him by Mrs.

Detty. There are more bound copies of the National Geographic up in this part of the world than anyone would believe. Even Lonergan-Logan has one, his is waterspotted and he got it at a Fire Sale for fifteen cents. I looked at Father Bailey's copy, hunting for water spots, but the light was bad. I thought if I occupied myself with a really diligent search for water spots that, this time, he would be the first to speak.

After a bit, I began to feel aggressive, and I said with elaborate politeness, "What's *your* idea of a blasphemous remark, Father Bailey?" I had several answers in mind for him, none of which he would be likely to invent, and my self-esteem began once more to unbutton. It takes very little to make me happy; someone should try.

He nodded, accepting the question, and he sat and thought about it for quite a while, his hands spread on his knees, looking at me as if I were a friendly hearthside fire. Finally, he answered, "How about 'Too good to be true'?"

I had not expected a cliché from him, and this was such an obvious cliché that I almost waved it aside like a gnat. Fortunately, I caught his meaning just in time, and the honest part of me (the part that I try to keep hidden in company) was impressed. I said, "I see," very slowly, not wanting to show that I was impressed but at the same time very anxious not to let him think that I had missed the point. I then said, "I see" again and added, "You're a good deal more hopeful than I am."

He said cheerfully, "Of course, I'm more hopeful than you are." After a moment, he added, "I'm also a great deal older, and I've had more time to think.—That's what you're trying to do, isn't it? Think?"

I could not deny it. I felt very embarrassed. I looked down at my hands and found a hangnail on one thumb which I industriously began to worry. I did not wish to look up, I did not wish to be impaled by those eyes which I feared were regarding me with professional wisdom and sincerity. I looked up anyhow, against my better judgment. Wrong again. Father Bailey was studying a paperknife as intently as I had been studying a hangnail. We both fidgeted away a slice of time before he finally said, "I presume you're looking for an answer, Richard?"

He had not called me Richard before today. He had not called me anything. I was dimly aware of being sucked into a relationship that I mistrusted—Drop around at Sunday service, my boy, I think you'll find we have some good thoughts for you to think. I remembered, defensively, that line of Thomas Paine's about "My own mind is my own church" but I rejected it, although it is a good line and I was once in love with revolutionaries. Some non-vulgar corner of my brain warned me that it wasn't relevant to my condition, and that I should not misuse a great writer.

I was left with the fact that Father Bailey had asked me outright if I was looking for an answer. Paine's hand may still have been upon me. I said, "Yes, I am," and it took more courage for me to say that (I was half-stammering) than to confess a hundred sins. Saying it, however, gave me back a little of my lately fled aggressiveness, and I added belligerently, "After all, who isn't looking for an answer? Except people like you."

"Me?"

I planted my hands on my knees and leaned forward, discovering too late that he must have abandoned his paperknife when I abandoned my hangnail and that we were now in identical postures. A pair of bookends, debating, but I wouldn't surrender. "You, of course." I spoke severely, feeling (thank God) quite keen-minded and logical again. "You've found your answer, haven't you?"

"In the Church?" said Father Bailey. "Heavens, no."

It was not what he was supposed to say, and I was once more off balance. He seemed to be able to do this to me with distressing ease. Like Codd, seducing the girl at the bar without touching her. Father Bailey and Codd simply follow their own lines of thought, while I travel down crazy roads, wave wildly at strangers, shout to them to wait for me, plead with them to communicate. The dialogue between Father Bailey and myself now appeared to have moved slightly off center. Was *I* to give *him* absolution? I fumbled through a mental card file—A for Absolution, B for Blessing . . . .

"I've confused you," he said apologetically. (C for Confusion—how obvious.) "I only meant that I came into the Church because I was looking for something. If I leave, it will be for the same reason."

"You might leave the Church?" I didn't believe him. He would freeze out there, in the cold dark.

"Certainly." He thought for a minute, shook his head slightly. "In fact, I almost did leave it when my own church burned down—the building, that is. I thought it might be a sign. I wanted to get away from all this up here, you know." I hadn't known, but I nodded, and he went on. "When I first came, I thought I would never stop cringing. One gets over that."

One did. I nodded again. I was beginning to feel very comfortable, man to man, the way I had felt with Detective Sloan. This autobiographical candor was very flattering, and I was flattered. I might have known it was loaded.

"I seldom cringe now," he said, "but sometimes—to avoid it, I suppose—I find myself wrapping the Church around me like a—"

"Like a shroud," I said. Too clever, too eager.

He didn't seem to notice me waving my aptitudes. "Like a quilt," he said. "Padded with good works. I find myself using service as a substitute for thought." He then said the one thing that he shouldn't have said to me. "Just as you do, Richard."

I don't know how he meant it, really. Maybe it was a philosophical remark, maybe it was a reminder about my letting

Ernie down, maybe it was a line from one of his Sunday sermons. But I think he meant it to hurt—that gentle old man in the clerical collar which licenses him to say anything he wants and to be holy while he's doing it.

Anyway, all of a sudden, I hated him. At least, I think I did. I got to my feet and stuck my hands into my pockets because they were shaking or something, and I said that I had already taken up too much of his time and that I had to go. I don't think I showed anything. I mean I wasn't bleeding on his carpet.

He took me to the door and he put his hand on my shoulder, just like Old Father Foundation himself. He told me reassuringly that things would be all right with Ernie. "With Mig too," he said.

I jerked away from him, and I answered as destructively as I knew how. "Ernie will go to hell, and Mig will go to hell, and, with your kind permission, maybe I'll go to hell too." I wanted a real obscenity, black as a slug, and I came up with a tin whistle. "It'll be better than your crappy Heaven," I said, and then I just stood there and waited for punishment.

He looked perfectly bewildered, and we stared at each other as if there was a fog in the hallway. His voice sounded thin, but all he did was ask one of his questions. "And what's *your* idea of Heaven, Richard?" (He wasn't laughing at me, was he? I don't think he was laughing at me.)

Two years ago, or even two hours, Richard wouldn't have answered. But my head was full of glass slivers, and I thought of everything that I want the world to be and everything that it isn't, and I shouted at him. "No one hurting anybody any more!" I shouted. "The goddam lion lying down with the goddam lamb!" And I ran down the stairs, and ran home.

24

It had been no part of Mig's plan that Mr. Harris should refer him to Mrs. Detty, who had the eyes and heart of a fish and who would never believe his tales about milk for Anna. Mr. Harris said it was a social-service matter and added stiffly that the Foundation could not be expected to provide nutritional supplements. "Food," he explained, irritating Mig who needed the explanation and hated needing it.

"You got it for Mrs. Ruiz," Mig said.

Richard Harris said sharply, "How did you know that?" and Mig said only that he knew a lot of things. He was sitting in Mr. Harris's chair and fingering Mr. Harris's kitchen knife which was used for opening letters and which had a very sharp blade. His host reached over and took it away from him. "I have to get food for Anna," Mig said, and added with careful emphasis, "One way or another." Then, letting his voice waver, he added, "She's sick."

"You said she wasn't."

"She wasn't sick then." Mig drew a deep sigh and said he would go to Father Bailey instead, and the effect was instantaneous. Mr. Harris said No, they would work it out somehow. He would talk to Anna and see that she went to a clinic.

A tiny snake of fear leaped. Mig told himself there was no reason why Anna should not go to a clinic, but he knew he would not let her. He might learn something he did not wish to know. He said hastily that the clinic was no good, that they were always too busy, people who only needed a little extra food would not get any help from a clinic.

"Then get a job and earn the food she needs."

"I tried," Mig said, lying with perfect sincerity. "I tried one place, he asked did I have a di-ploma from high school. I tried another place, he wanted to know where I live. I told him and he said he don't hire no kids from there. I should," said Mig piously, "have lied."

"No, no. I'll talk to a friend, maybe someone downtown. Or I'll talk to Mrs. Detty myself, and she can talk to Anna."

The little snake leaped again, causing Mig to take refuge in an absolute truth. He said sullenly, "She don't like me."

"Mrs. Detty? She likes Anna."

"She don't like me. She'd try to take Anna away." He looked around the room and beheld that Mr. Harris had everything—possessions, a place to put them, a job, money and power. He made one more statement, poetically perfect in its aim. "Anna could die," he said. "Like a bird." He looked down at the floor.

Mr. Harris said heavily, "I'll see what I can do."

Mig ran down the steps, heady with success.

Ernie was waiting for him at the corner, must have followed him here. He was through with Ernie and merely gave him a look of contempt and brushed past. The sallow face went muddily pink, and for a moment of human outrage Ernie was a hero and nearly chose independence, but the habit of Mig was too much for him. He ran after this friend who was also his emperor. "Mig!"

Mig turned and responded, savagely and at length. Ernie backed off like a whipped puppy, murmuring and holding his thumbs discreetly. He was, by nature, a friendly creature, and he had never before known such terrible loneliness as he had endured since Mig had shut him out. With Mig and Anna, he had a place, however small. He had been allowed to share the stolen TV at least once a week, allowed to look at Anna, allowed to idolize Mig. His bone, his basket and his blanket. The street had not really changed since that idiot moment of fear and fury when he had used his teeth against the Law, but around Ernie there was now a circle of emptiness that echoed and was very cold.

He said "Mig" again, forlornly.

Mig spat, less in disgust or anger than in artistic elaboration, but Ernie, who could not know this, turned on his heel and went away. The feeling of pleasure to be gained by hitting such helplessness drained out of Mig completely, and he stood on the sidewalk and knew he had been a fool and had lost more than he had gained. There were other slaves to be had, but Ernie was not just a slave.

It was an auspicious time to run into the drunk woman who lived next door to that Mrs. Ruiz for whom Mr. Harris had produced so many luxuries. Mig knew her vaguely, knew that she came from Queens but was not perfectly clear where Queens was. Her face was not quite as red as it usually was but looked rainstreaked and mottled, and her jerkings and mouthings were unpleasant to watch. She was wearing a pink dress with a cherry-colored coat, crusty with age, greasy with dirt, and bedroom slippers that slurred behind her feet. She did not often come out on the street—only when, sick with compulsive need, she went to buy her bottled baby and nestle it home. Some day she would simply lurch into the gutter, fall and never get up again.

She greeted Mig and stuck out a red swollen paw at him, and he stopped when he saw that it held a little, brown, busted purse. She smiled cloudily, announcing that he was to help her because she was on her way home to Queens and she had lost the bottle that someone had given her. She groped for the someone's name, and then said "The father" with uncertain satisfaction.

"Father Bailey?" It seemed unlikely.

She asked who Father Bailey was, and then, without waiting for an answer, she began to fumble at Mig's jacket, groping toward his pocket. He pulled away, and she said, plainly hurt, that she only wanted him to take her purse. There was a bottle in it, she said, and it was going to be taken away from her. Her eyes filled with such sadness that they overflowed.

He accepted the purse, assuring himself that he was doing her a real kindness. Somebody else would come along, take her money and leave her empty-handed and full of terror, in the middle of the street and with her home lost. He, Mig, knew exactly what to do—buy her a bottle of cheap wine and take her back to her own doorway to drink it. He slipped two neat fingers inside the purse and felt folding money. *Two* bottles of wine. The rest of the money (which meant most of it) would repay him for his kindness. He would be able to tell Anna how kind he had been, and a part of his mind glanced around for Ernie to complete his audience.

"Dear, dear boy," the woman said, fondly and clearly, as if she had reached somewhere back into her past and found a boy who had truly been dear once.

He slipped a hand under her elbow and told her to come with him. He was almost courtly, and she gave a faint snuffle of comfort and leaned against him, murmuring softly, not so lonesome now and going to have her drink which would make her less lonesome than ever. She nodded almost cheerfully at this kindly street which had given her such a handsome boy to take care of her and which would, very soon, give her oblivion.

25

There is nothing wrong with my friend Father Bailey except that his calling has made him self-righteous. Looking back, I have no idea why I got so angry. It doesn't matter now. All is forgiven.

I ran into Ernie this morning and presented him with a five-dollar bill and some good advice. He will interpret the money as a reward for biting a cop, but actually I gave it to him so that he would have to stand still and accept my well-prepared lecture. Maybe he would have listened to me anyway. He is a sad little creature, like a weasel as Mig is like a fox.

I live in a jungle certainly, but not the kind of jungle I was led to expect. A determined, stolid daily life persists among the marauding tarantulas, the ropy liana vines, the swamp miasma, the night terrors. The boa constrictors here prey on small animals who scream at a touch, but they leave the tigers respectfully alone. With the first jungle rain, the gutters turn into clotted sewers, and the crocodiles lie in them, blinking. The vultures are, unsuitably, as gaudy as peacocks, and the jackals have small soft feet but you can smell them coming. Occasionally there is a flash of real beauty, which I seldom see except after it has happened.

Originally, this jungle was established by white rabbits, who proliferated and underwent mutational changes. Some of them stayed small and lived in their rabbit holes (equably or in continual panic, according to the health of their genes), and some of them became group rabbits and attached themselves to wholesome organizations. Some took to religion, and some to drugs. A few latecomers have found themselves domiciled in Foundations, but these categories are, of course, exceptions to the Jungle Law which says that no one can escape. Herded together by elite tribesmen, all the animals recognize this Law. They rise occasionally, having studied how to band together, but their riots abort and the tribesmen (who write dissertations) tell us reassuringly that the jungle animals only loot their own dens and burn their own harvests. This makes them homeless and hungry, and, of course, it is all their fault.

Comforting, isn't it?

What I was trying to tell Ernie with my crazy five-dollar bill was that, occasionally, good things ($5.00) happen even to bad things (Ernie), quite unexpectedly and out of a clear sky. My five dollars is a personal act of gratitude—not to Ernie for biting a cop, but to a cop for not clubbing Ernie. Biting is a clear and present danger, and it unqualifiedly comes under the heading of "resisting arrest." I do not know how the cop went about pulling in his savage minnow—carried him under one arm probably, a limp pale body full of terror because of what he had done and certainly expecting a beating. I like to tell myself that the bitten cop understood that Ernie has had enough pain and humiliation in his sad itchy life without needing more. If I thought that, I would feel better about Ernie . . . .

No, I feel fine about Ernie. We've got a great thing going, Ernie and me. That five-dollar bill was my own money, not expense-account-for-miscellaneous-disasters. Ernie could legitimately be certified as a miscellaneous disaster, but that five bucks was my own five bucks.

As to Mig, he has been here again, begging milk for his Anna as if he was a dried-up mother cat with one kitten. I suspect her of going hungry so she can buy the things he wants to eat, and, as he is a monument of selfishness, it is something new for him to have looked at her and realized that she is undernourished. And he *has* tried to go out and get a job, so this may be the point where I could approach Codd and ask for help. Just to get Mig out of this damned closed-up world, this junkies' dustheap, for eight hours a day might make all the difference. He cares about Anna, I swear he cares about her, his voice was quite gentle.

Of course, all his Anna really needs is some vitamin C, a week in the Bahamas, a dozen red roses, and a mother.

I suppose I am leaning on Anna now in my mind, the way I have been leaning on Jeannie. The difference is that I want to do things for Anna, and I want Jeannie to do things for me. There is, if the truth be known (and it is known, for all my dodging it) a massive loneliness building up inside me, and I need a woman, not so much to lie in bed with (you can speak freely, Richard, you are among friends) as one to hold onto very tightly. I cannot get at Jeannie, and it would certainly not be fair to Anna to hold tightly to anything so fragile, as Ellyn held tightly to me. (She did?)

If anyone doesn't believe that my soul is sick, he need only take a look at that last paragraph, riddled with parentheses. Parentheses are the last infirmity of a noble mind. Can I, however, contemplate Ellyn tonight without this coward's recourse to parenthetical expressions? Poor Ellyn. She probably wanted from me what I want from Jeannie, and it must have been a blow when my parentheses sprang to meet hers, but only back to back.

)(())(()

Hate, love, hate, love. I have created a new psycho-religious symbol. I shall take it to Father Bailey and have it blessed—a remark which makes me realize that it is not true that I am no longer angry with him. I thoroughly hated him at our last meeting. He makes me more restless and angry than anyone else has ever made me in my entire lifetime. Compared to Father Bailey, the fair Ellyn was a sedative, a tranquilizer, a baby's pacifier. He enrages me, and I keep going back to him, out of some idiot conviction that he knows something that I do not know. Which I want to know.

But that's all there is to church-going anyway, isn't it? You be the shepherd, and I'll be the sheep. Baaaa!

Where does he get the right to tell me that I am using service as a substitute for thought? He said it about himself too, but it isn't true and he knows it. It was only his clever-professor way of closing the gap between us. (Professor Blount used to do that very well, I know all the old men's little tricks. And damn the parentheses! No one is looking at my parentheses. At my present rate of literary creativity, no one ever will.) And while I am lynching Father Bailey and Professor Blount, I would also like to lynch that bearded young leopard at Codd's party, who had published a novel, and who bent to me, leaned to me, so politely. "What do you do, little man, in your little world?" "I write," said I, beaming and manly. And Ellyn pulled back the corner of the wall-to-wall carpet under which I had crawled, and she dug me out of a crack and took me home to my own home and we spent a memorable night trying to destroy each other.

And *I* was the one who said to Father Bailey—my parting words—that Heaven to me would be people not hurting each other.

You are old, Father Bailey, and it is not kind, it is not kind to make me look at myself. I have been going around doing good deeds, binding up wounds, pressing five-dollar bills into eager hands, running little errands for little foundations, perfectly satisfied. I had a corner here with no mirrors in it.

It's just after midnight. If I call Jeannie, she will not answer. If I call God, He will not be in. I could not be kind to Ellyn until I was sure that she would be kind to me, and so—on my own terms, those words I flung at Father Bailey—I threw away one more small chance at salvation.

But I don't believe in salvation, do I?

26

In the sober days, in the days when she had lived in her own house in Queens, with its own backyard, white iron ducks on the lawn and a quiet husband, she was Mrs. Peters. She had been a pretty girl, a biddable wife, a lively young widow, but the coming-on of age had been beyond her capacity and alcohol had offered to give her back her youth. It was as simple as that.

Her vice was economical enough, needing only cheap wine not whiskey, and the money that came monthly from her husband's estate preserved her in a kind of genteel wretchedness. He had meant it to preserve her in self-respect and comfort, but she had lost track of such things long ago, sliding deeper every day into the swamp of herself.

Across the hallway from her lived Mrs. Ruiz, forever shrilling at her husband, bulging with babies, hostile. Mrs. Peters was afraid of Mrs. Ruiz, as she was afraid of everyone now except Father Bailey and the young man called Mig who had lately come into her life and helped her. Once she had had a son, but the son had fathered two children and, with them and his meemy-marmy little thin wife, he had moved to New Jersey and did not want to see her. The young man Mig could be her son if he wished to be, and his kindness in getting wine for her was a kindness that was altogether new and hopeful. She leaned one day on her dirty sink and peered into her dirty mirror and was able to find in that spoiled image some memory of the girl she had been. Mig's girl was named Anna; he had told her so, shyly. Her own name was Ann, but she did not tell him that, keeping it as a precious secret to hug to a lonely breast. Anna and Ann, Mig's two girls. Sometimes she was his mother, and that was a comfort to her too. She thought dimly of telling Father Bailey about Mig, because he would be glad to know that someone was looking after her or that she was looking after someone, but for the time being she wanted to keep Mig for her own. He was a private place where she could rest her poor, tired and old head, a head that hummed all the time like a top and spun endlessly without really moving.

Mig, in his turn, accepted his role. He supplied services to the old creature—buying her liquor, steering her home, supporting her sodden body, prying her loose from her own front steps when she wound in bitter fatigue around the broken iron railing. For this, he charged a very high fee from the brown purse, but he did not steal from her, because he did not steal from anybody. He left that to the Ernies who were useful when they were clever, and expendable when they were caught.

Still, there were problems about Ernie, and one of these was that Anna missed him, not from love (Mig knew extremely well where Anna's love lay) but from some vague comfort that he gave her. Mig could have ignored this, if there had not been inside himself something equally vague so that, from time to time, he tolerated Ernie's overtures, cutting them short only when they became too hopeful. And, even then, he did not quite feel the satisfaction he had counted on in being so powerful. He chewed all this over in his mind, turning it about uneasily, faintly restless, but on the whole Mrs. Peters had come into his world at an ideal moment from the point of view of his income and of his ego.

This was especially true because Mr. Harris, instead of supplying money, seemed determined to supply employment.

It was not that Mig was altogether opposed to a job of his own, if it was a suitable one (the princeling in him often had visions), but the kind of job that Mr. Harris talked about was not that kind of job at all. Eight hours a day in some warehouse, eight hours a day delivering groceries or running errands, eight hours a day saying yes-ma'am and no-sir to fat customers, fat with money and power—that was not for him.

"You could get out of here," Mr. Harris had said, meaning the street.

Mig ducked his head and said sadly that this was his *home,* sending out instant tendrils of possession like a sucking vine.

"You could go to school," Mr. Harris said.

No, said Mig, he could not, because he knew nothing. He did not add that his hands went clammy at the thought and his stomach cramped. His ignorance was his terror, and the smallest mention of education sent something screaming in his mind, screaming that he could not read, only the simplest words. The other words would not let him in, and books were black nothings. He had even torn up the instruction book that came with the television set, and he would have torn up Anna's magazine too, but she had hid it. Smart little cat, stupid little cat . . . .

He held onto himself and tried not to yell at Mr. Harris for having suggested school. He could do without Mr. Harris now, if he wanted to, now that he had Mrs. Peters. He did not really like Mrs. Peters at all, but he cherished her because she was money in the bank. Once, he had brought her home, back to his own room, when her gaspings and stumblings had been more than he could manage. She lay on his bed, flat out with her mouth open and her eyes staring and her face red. He had thought she was going to die on him, but Anna had stroked the red forehead and patted the spongy cheeks, and after a while Mrs. Peters had opened her eyes and she had not died. Anna had covered her with the blanket and sat beside her for two hours, looking into her face as if she had found her lost doll.

When Mrs. Peters had rested long enough to be able to use her own feet again, Mig took her back to her own place, and he saw to it that she never used his bed or saw his girl again. He did not quite know why. If you looked at the woman, she was nothing but a lump of old flesh, and Anna had acted just the same to him afterwards as she always did.

Only, for just a moment, he had got the feeling that there might not always be enough of Anna, skinny Anna, to go around.

27

A check for $100.00, made out to cash, stares at me from my bed. It is pale blue, and the name of J. Coddington Woodhill is imprinted in one corner. I am watching it very closely from where I sit at my typewriter, and it neither moves nor blinks. It is bloodless. It has no eyes, no mouth, only a skeleton jaw fitted with grinning teeth.

Professor Blount would tell me that I am pressing the metaphor too far. I do this sometimes, but I am only wringing my metaphors instead of wringing my hands. With no counsel from professors to see me through this evening of my confusions, I shall have to take relief where I can find it. Besides, it is all true. There is a pale-blue skeleton staring at me from my bed. Until I laid it there, I thought it was human and warm and lovely, like a biddable and beddable girl, a Jeannie of kindness.

"No strings attached," Codd said generously, and he tore the check neatly out of a checkbook that has his initials on it in gold. And then he got up from his desk—a courteous man who had already given more time than he could afford out of a busy day to an old college friend—and I found myself going out the door with his friendly hand on my shoulder, babbling my gratitude, the hundred-dollar check lustrous in my hand.

The glow of my success lasted me all the way home, lasted

until this moment when the check stares at me from across the room—a paper rectangle worth $100.oo and costing exactly nothing. I wish now that I had torn it up carefully and put the pieces on his mahogany desk and walked out of his office.

I wanted him to give Mig a job. The money he gave me instead is hush-money, leave-me-alone-money, don't-get-me-involved. He took me in beautifully, and I thanked him from the bottom of my humble cotton-pickin' heart, mumbling my exit, sniffing his check like a bouquet of roses.

I might have foreseen that he would dodge my plan for him to provide a job for my ghetto derelict. One never knows, does one, what one of these underprivileged lads might do to bring shame and disgrace on a fine old Park Avenue firm? One might find oneself responsible for a tramp-boy, a delinquent precocious man-child, a terrifying unknown quantity called human. I can taste the bile of my bitterness now, and I shall spit it out and be done with Codd forever, cash his check and use it for Anna and other neglected, tender causes.

Or I *could* spit it out, if only I had no memory and no sense of justice. Look, comrades, how neat it all is—a mathematical formula of absolute precision. Codd is to Mig as Richard was to Ernie. Who can blame Codd for not wanting to get involved? His life is a world away from these streets. Who can fail to blame me? My life is here.

I wrote that rather well, I think. It has a sort of iambic-pentameter power. If I were writing a novel (that second novel I am so afraid of, the first one having been stillborn) , I could incorporate my fine sentence structures into its perceptive chapters. I could put my human frailty on paper to enlighten mankind. Instead, I sit here and watch it twitch, and then I put it down in this five-finger exercise . . . . . . No, actually, very simply, not just being self-conscious with that string of dots, I think I *am* trying to be decently honest. After all, I'm a hundred dollars ahead, and I can use it to help Anna and others who need help, and it is quite understandable that Codd would not wish to become involved in my subterranean world and its finny inhabitants. That excuses him; it does not excuse me. I suppose I have to be this self-analytical? I suppose I have to knot the rope around my neck and hang myself on the hook in the dark corner? I couldn't just say, "Sleep well, Richard, a hundred bucks to the good—how clever you are to have such a wealthy friend"?

But God damn my wealthy friend! He would bed a girl without thinking of any consequences, why won't he hire a seventeen-year-old boy who comes well recommended——

Yes, I did recommend Mig, didn't I? I did recommend this boy, knowing that I cannot trust him as far as my doorway, this boy who is as clever as a cat and who fawns on me and purrs and has no heart and no scruples. I did imply to Codd—did I not?—that this was a trustworthy lad, bright as a button, true as steel, a veritable Galahad, an investment in humanity no less. Richard the Lionhearted, Richard the Spellbinder.

All right. I've made my confession. Flagellation should be carried just so far. That check on my bed is simply a check. Because I despise it now, I may misuse it, so I shall take it to Father Bailey and ask him to see what he can do, discreetly, for Anna.

Neat, isn't it? I can do this sort of thing standing on my head. Father Bailey gives me absolution and takes over my responsibility, at one and the same time. I wonder if Codd would care to offer *me* a job? I think I could write advertising for fraudulent banks, squeeze vitamin-C benefits from ersatz oranges, praise corporations from Whom all blessings flow.

If I were lying on my bed with Jeannie, I would put Codd's check under the mattress and never have to think of it again. It would survive there, a piece of worthless paper, and some day it would distress Codd's accountant. The bank statement would not be in balance; the sky is falling, Chicken Little.

Jeannie, the sky is falling. Jeannie, if I could put my head in your lap like a unicorn finding a fair lady, I could tell you my very private thoughts. Such as, if I marry, I shall almost certainly be faithful. Such as, if I could unclench my fists, I could weep like a child.

Jeannie.

Jeannie?

No responses.

I am lonely. I want some kind of an answer. I want so much to believe in something. I suppose that is why I keep going back to Father Bailey, like a puppy to a gnawed bone, thinking he will give me what I am looking for. He says he hasn't found it in the Church, he says he might leave the Church. I don't believe that somehow. It's easy enough to talk about the storm when the roof over your head is as neat and tight as his. I resent his smugness, but I have to admit that he is not altogether smug. He is, I suppose, a questing man, full of faith. I am a questing man, full of doubts.

There I am, with my Great Thoughts again. Someone should bind me in limp leather, preserving the chasm between what I say and what I do. When I was in college, the most profound thing I encountered was that line of Yeats—"sick with desire and fastened to a dying animal." For me, it was earthshaking. It summed up all human history and all morality. I hung over that line, fascinated and revolted, and when I had forced myself to accept it, I thought I had arrived at a total honesty, a sublime (and sublimated) acknowledgment of things as they are. I kept that line by me as if it were an amulet, telling myself that it is rock-bottom. If you accept what it says, you accept total disaster and know you can't do anything about it. Not fatalism, not despair, something beyond and much more terrible.

I believe that I really enjoyed it in a way—me, out there at the edge of the universe, shivering healthily in that icy wind, a college junior swinging the comets by their tails. I thumped my chest and I understood Yeats and, by God, I was a man who could face Life! Or—braver still—I could face the knowledge that the desire and the dying animal were all there was to life, not looking back and not looking forward as I strode along my glorious Siegfried highway.

So when did I start to ask myself if Yeats' line was really the whole of revealed truth? When did I start to ask if there might be something more? Father Bailey thinks that there is, but he doesn't say that he has found it—just that it's there and that it can be found. Father Bailey embarrasses me somewhat, although it is true that I keep going back to him.

At any rate, my typewriter has once more drawn the poison. I can look at the blue check lying on my bed and see nothing more than a hundred-dollar bonus which can be usefully converted and cheerfully spent.

I have just remembered something that Codd said to me this afternoon. He asked me how the writing was going (old boy, old boy, old boy), and my evasive answer was designed to lead him down sunlit alleys and not let him see the dead ends. Respectful layman, he said that he knew enough about writers to realize that they didn't always want to discuss their work-in-progress (one hyphenated word, he must have learned it from that leopard who loaned Ellyn to me). I suppose I looked mysterious, because he then gave me a fine lecherous look, man to man, and said, "How's your private life?" It wasn't a question I felt inclined to field, so I was silent, and after a moment he gave a fractional shrug and changed the subject. I am not sure whether he interpreted my silence as vacuum or repletion, kindergarten or graduate school.

But, looking back, I see now that my private life would shock him—my really private life. Men like him who are happy to tell you all about their sexual conquests would die of shame if you asked if they believed in God. Perhaps that's why I keep

149

going back to Father Bailey? He embarrasses me, but I don't embarrass him. I find this restful.

For the moment, at any rate, I am serene. If I ask Father Bailey to administer Codd's hundred dollars, it will not be because I am trying to escape responsibility. It will be because he is a wise, kind, experienced and trustworthy man. I really think I hate him. If I told him I was going to become an atheist, he would probably tell me pleasantly that I don't have enough energy for it.

I don't know that, of course. He might just say, "Go ahead, my boy, and God bless you." Which would give him, as usual, the last word.

28

Sometimes, at night, Anna dreamed about her mother. There was always a picture of the Holy Family in the dream, and the stove with two burners, and her mother's wide hips and black dresses. There was her face too sometimes, but not often. Anna was a little afraid of seeing her mother's face.

The night that Mig had promised to take her home and then had made his promise useless because he was not a part of it—that night, Anna had dreamed a mother with a face that was whole and smiling but belonged to someone else. Anna knew herself wicked and supposed herself to be damned, finding in this such hopelessness that every day drove her closer to the moment when decision would be not choice but despair.

Once, she dreamed that the baby had died and that Mig bought a tiny coffin for it. Once, she dreamed that Mama Kraus lay dead of a broken neck at the foot of a staircase. The worst dream of all was when she woke in her mother's arms and found herself looking up into Mama Kraus's fat-imbedded eyes.

Anna came out of that dream with her own eyes wild and staring in the dark room, her fingers taping her mouth shut against the liberating scream. Mig breathed peacefully beside her, but she dared not touch or wake him, and when she finally wept, she wept very silently.

Wearily, stoically, she accepted being more alone all the time. In this world that was not her world at all, she had never been able to make any real friends, although Mrs. Detty clucked at her from time to time and Mr. Harris had a way of looking at her which made her feel disloyal, as if she was not entirely Mig's but that there might be places where she belonged to herself. Lately, Mr. Harris had been bringing her things like powdered milk (which she ate, not too happily, with a spoon because, although she knew it was good for her, she did not know about adding water) and sometimes fruit which she saved for Mig who ate it greedily and brightly like a very small boy.

Once, on the street, she met Cassy and Irmalee and Angel who had got money together from somewhere and were going to the dance hall, an unknown quantity to Anna but connected with lights and music. They invited her to go with them, and she said she would ask Mig. They told her very plainly that they did not want Mig, and she was never asked anywhere again. Without Mig, of course, she would not have gone anyway, but she liked having been asked and supposed that their reason for not wanting Mig was that Angel might not like it. Anna knew about Angel and Cassy and Irmalee, as everyone knew about them and nobody cared, and if she made any judgment at all, it was a pitying one because Angel was not much of a man and Mig was. One of the reasons she no longer liked to dream about her mother was that Mig hated her mother, and Anna thought loyally that she ought to share his hate. Since she could not, she wished for dreamless nights.

In truth, Anna was beginning to dry up entirely. There was no earth to nourish her torn roots, no stream to water them, no sun to reach for. She thought numbly that she was dying of the child inside her, and perhaps after all that was what she ought to do? Knowledgeable beyond knowledge, she knew she would go to Mama Kraus and she did not think she would survive the going.

God would punish her in her own death, and that was really her only hope. Some day she would stop running, and His hand would fall. In that faint comfort of certain doom, she survived from hour to hour, two lives in one body and no life at all in her very young heart.

As for Mig, he was restless.

Mr. Harris had given up the unpleasant talk about school. He did not even mention any more the possibility of that threatened "job downtown" which would bind him eight hours a day to the unknown, to a place where he would be forever hiding his ignorance of so many things, pretending to understand what he did not understand, to read what he could not read. Once, when he was nine years old, something had suddenly gone wrong with Mig's ears and he was afraid to tell anybody. His head had seemed to swell into a great balloon of listening, and he guessed frantically at words he could no longer hear, and his own voice made a sound like wood. The deafness had vanished as abruptly as it came, and he was nine-year-old lord of himself again within a week, but the memory still frightened him and he would not go where his ignorance could isolate him as his ears once had.

Here, on his own street, he knew more than Anna, could read more words than Ernie, felt superior to Mrs. Peters lurching toward her bottles. If he had a lot of money, of course, he would take it and go away and leave everything behind. He was not clear where he would go, but the money would buy him the world he needed—sun and success and the blonde that he still dreamed of casually. Once, in his golden dream, he was so rich that he even sent money back to Anna to take care of her.

In the meantime, Mrs. Peters was a small steady source, greatly enhanced by her growing dependency. There was a rumor that she had money in a bank somewhere, and he thought he would find out about this and, if it was true, make himself even more useful. She had a son somewhere too, and she was bitter toward him and toward his wife. Mig told her that she should not let that son get any of her money, and she listened to his good advice and nodded her drunken head to the drunken rhythm inside her, pressing his hand and calling him her real son which was what he wanted her to do.

But things moved much too slowly, and his restlessness and boredom grew. When, after an absence, the men came back to their room again (so that, once more, he and Anna were told to stay away at certain hours of the day), Mig took careful note of their new look of prosperity and began to think that there might be some way he could share it. At no risk to himself, of course. There was no reason why he should put his neck into their noose. If he ever took their orders, he would see to it that someone else carried them out.

And so, inevitably, he forgave Ernie. He had meant to banish him forever, but now he snapped his fingers and brought him back, grateful and eager. Ernie had learned his lesson, and Ernie came to heel like a good dog. Mig said, no, he had nothing in mind for him, just wanted him around, and the pinched hopeful little face swelled with a very simple joy.

In a way, Mig meant it. Ernie's return pleased Anna, and at the moment it pleased Mig to please her. It made him feel that he still controlled her life, and he needed to feel this. There were times now when Anna roused in him a faint sickness that was very close to fear.

29

We had a riot up here yesterday, cooled it with expertise so
quickly that I felt nothing but confusion. Everyone seemed to
be going through motions, like a patriotic polka. Somebody
yelled, somebody threw a beer can, somebody screeched, somebody threw a rock, somebody called the cops, everybody went
so thin you could have hid them behind lamp posts. Cops
stood their ground, rioters stood their ground, a trash can burst
mysteriously into flame like a phoenix, Apaches danced so
beautifully that I was dazzled. I saw war feathers and heard
tomtoms. A baby waddled too close and scorched its budding
nose, everybody died fantastically, falling like leaves into pat-
terns of anguish and despair, but the baby lived, squalling, and
everybody resurrected and its mother or its great-aunt or its
great-great-grandmother with a beard clutched its screams and
rocked its lullaby. And no one did anything at all except vanish
very skillfully, and the cops sighed and went home, and I went
home and sighed.

The report I am writing for the Foundation is not quite like
that. I am seeking to convey to my employers, intellectually,
that the work being done here is bearing fruit. If the natives
turn and rend me tomorrow night, burn up the street and set
the Fire Department ablaze, strangled in its own hoses, I shall
have to amend my report. I amend reports very gracefully.

155

Sometimes I wonder what the Foundation does with the paper dolls that I send them. Is there a Dorothy, a Rose, a Viola, a Desdemona perhaps, assigned to filing *Harris, Richard?*

Not a Jeannie. There are no Jeannies any more.

Did I tell you that, Professor Blount? The telephone and I have made our peace at last. Jeannie has gone away, to Washington—not even to Washington, D.C. which I can just conceive but to the State of Washington which is almost the same thing as dying. One more escape route has closed, and there is a killing frost on my dear meadow. This morning I told Father Bailey about her going away because I had to tell somebody, not to waste my cherished young-man sorrow, and Mrs. Detty is downtown today, swindling a bank or founding a dynasty or appearing in court. She is often in court, and I am never able to find out exactly why. I presume she likes it there, the way she likes that bathroom mirror which she cannot leave. Anyway, she was not around for me to tell her about Jeannie, so I told my old friend and father confessor who said "Your girl?" I said sullenly, no, she was not my girl, and I would have gone on to display my wounds but I sensed that the subject had failed to grip him. How often I find I do not fascinate others as much as I fascinate myself. Us knights-at-arms need damsels, the way Mrs. Detty needs her mirror. Veneration, not sex. I am on the verge of yet one more great thought, which is that sex is a good deal easier to come by than respect.

I am sorry to be the one to bring you this message, Giovanni Giacomo Casanova de Seingalt, but perhaps you will sleep all the better for it. Good night, then, and pleasant dreams.

Good night, Jeannie, good night, good night.

. . . . . .

However, it is only eight o'clock, and I am not Casanova and I am not a little boy. I have no one to telephone to any longer, but I do have other matters to think about. There is Anna, for example. Something is wrong with Anna these days, she looks like wax. And something is wrong with Geo. Lonergan-Logan too. He has not asked me for help in three weeks' time, and he rarely leaves his room. He is deathly afraid of being ill, so I cannot suggest his going to a clinic. Mrs. Ruiz hints that he has taken to drink or drugs or harems, but she showers everyone with her careless slander and has even been known to accuse the Welfare Commissioner of unnatural practices. And she may be right because she sincerely believes that his Department would be willing to send Lonergan-Logan to the Bahamas for his health, which would be an unnatural practice indeed. Mrs. Detty, by the way, agrees with Mrs. Ruiz about this, although she is more realistic and says that it is not a likely procedure. I am surrounded by mad people.

And, once again, I see that I have raised the monocle of humor to my supercilious eye. I turn these people into after-dinner conversation pieces, tailored to amuse. Dear quaint Mrs. Ruiz! Dear black Mrs. Detty! How good they all are on this street of mine, as good as gold—barring, of course, their minor lapses into vice, corruption, mayhem, murder, addiction, bestiality and sloth. The view from my monocle—gleeful, cool—changes them just enough to be bearable, keeps them at a distance in their exotic frame, faintly lovable, wholly absurd, savages but friendly ones.

On the other hand, they *are* friendly, and I do love them from time to time. They can exhibit such a sweet and terrible goodness that I respond to it as I might to physical pain and find myself holding my breath against its anguish. They are all so self-destructive that it seems childish even to talk of right and wrong, or of good and bad. Anna is good, like a little dog, but like a little dog she would kill if she had to for her beloved master. And Mig, who I believe not to be good, would never kill for anyone. He would simply not endanger himself in that way, and so he would remain technically chaste while Anna sinned.

However, I may have that wrong. Anna would not kill for Mig, but she would die for him. I suppose that Mig would just stand by and let her die.

This is what Father Bailey calls my "automatic assumption" about Mig—that the evil in him will automatically dominate the good. Obviously, Father Bailey doesn't think I have the right to judge anybody's soul, and good Father Bailey is quite correct, of course. But we don't live with their souls as neighbors, and it is not their souls that my Foundation (How firm a Foundation! Oh, do be funny, Richard, I adore you when you're funny)—It is not their souls that my Foundation pays me to look after. Healthy minds in healthy bodies, my boy. Wipe out the demon whiskey and the demon drug and the demon sex and move into a brave new world.

Sometimes, like tonight, I just get so damn lonely. All day long I lift one foot and I put it down, and then I lift the other foot and I put it down, and I inch along these cruddy streets and I don't think I am really achieving anything at all. I might be better off working in a factory or writing another bad novel or climbing a mountain or marrying an ambitious woman who would type my Ph.D. thesis for me and mother my children and GIVE ME MEALS ON TIME. Once I had a friend, and he was a good friend, who had found the answer and wanted to share it with me. The answer was drugs, of course, hard and cool, and he was something of an artist in them and so convincing that I almost bought his life style. (Dear dead days when I could romantically call a hard-on a pet name like "life style," instead of seeing something human jerking in a gutter.) Only, one day, quiet-eyed, a little slurry in his speech, obviously enormously happy, my good friend told me that he loved his drugs because they gave him a sense of possibilities.

Christ! who needs a drug for that? I was born with a sense of possibilities, what I want is a sense of fulfillment. The difference between me and Father Bailey is that he believes in some kind of fulfillment, and I don't any more. I used to believe in it. In fact, isn't that why I came here—good works, my novel, the committed life? Perhaps I need a good kind church to minister to me, after all.

But Father Bailey said that he might leave his church. And, a few paragraphs back, Richard Harris put down in black and white—without thinking about it, without beating his breast, without self-pity—that he had written a bad novel.

There is hope for us all?

30

Mama Kraus was expecting her. Mama Kraus had fat hands but she knew her job, and Anna kept herself alive through all of it by thinking of the presents that Mig had given her. There was the magazine, the candy bar, the cross on its chain, the magazine, the candy bar, the cross on its chain, the magazine, the candy bar——

"That's all, little Anna," Mama Kraus said. "Pay me when you have the money. We're friends?" She said it again. "We're friends?"

Anna whispered yes, she would pay. It was over. She lived. Mama Kraus's dog came from the other side of the room, and she sat up vaguely and reached out to pat it, but it moved away, growling. "And don't tell anybody what you've done," said Mama Kraus, sounding like the dog.

The litany of the magazine, the candy bar, the cross, changed inside her head to a new litany. I will pay you, I will not tell, I will pay you, I will not tell. She carried this down the stairs and out into the street, and when someone said querulously, "You all right, girl, you sure you all right?" she said "I will pay you," and when someone else called her name twice, she said "I will not tell." She took her body home and Mig was not there, so she laid it on the bed and pulled the blanket over it. It was silent, chilled, indifferent, and when it slept, it slept totally.

There was one small piece of sunlight on the floor, which moved across the room slowly and became smaller and paler as it moved. When Mig came into the room, it had gone entirely, and the floor which was dirty but might have been dirtier had a gray-amethyst look. He was moving very lightly, almost prancing, because Mrs. Peters had given him ten dollars for an eighty-nine-cent bottle of wine. It seemed he had only to move his wrist lazily and put out his slim hand, palm up. She was an old fool, almost boringly easy.

He said "Anna," and she turned over stiffly and raised heavy eyelids. She looked like a rag and her smile was a ghost, and he thought that he would keep his good news to himself for a while. He lay down and took her hand into his. It was a small hand, more like a paw, a little clammy. The fingers curled inside his, and he heard her sigh his name and felt her head against his shoulder. For once, he did not pull her to him or push her away, but let her rest there quietly. When she said "I will pay you," he thought she was having a dream.

31

Duty-bound, I went to see Geo. Lonergan-Logan this morning. I met a gigantic rat on his staircase, and it stared at me for a bleak moment, bristle-whiskered, and then disappeared into a gouged hole in its wall. I stood there with the sweat pouring off my heroic body, and then I went on up the stairs, watching where I put my feet.

When I knocked on Logan's door, no one answered. I shook the doorknob and it nearly came off in my hands, and then, because the rat had seemed like a premonition of disaster, I started to hammer on the gray blistered panel. The door across the way opened at once, and a knotty black head came out, looked me up and down, and withdrew like the rat. I yelled, and the door opened again and the head came out again. It was like being in a puppet show. I pulled my voice down and said "Please" very politely, in case there was a knife in the hands beyond that head. I then asked the head if it thought that Mr. Logan was in, exactly the way I would have asked Codd's secretary if Mr. J. Coddington Woodhill was seeing clients. Inside the cage of my fear, there was at least a small defiant squeak of laughter.

The head said something completely foreign and incomprehensible, but it neither roared nor hissed as jungle voices often do, and its mouth went into an O with the corners up. I liked that. I could have stood there indefinitely, chatting without any language, knowing that O-mouth to be smiling, knowing the rat to be in the wall and not on the staircase, and not having to know yet whether or not Logan was lying dead in his bed, dead for a week because I had not come to see him and nobody else cared.

A little whine of music came from the room behind the head, and I thought maybe there was a cobra in there being charmed by a flute, but then I realized it must be a radio. The surrealist Tiffany-glass jigsaw inside my head began to come together, and I said briskly, "Do you know if Logan's in?"

The head disappeared, and the door closed forever.

I shrugged. I lifted my right hand and rapped my knuckles on Logan's door. When there was still no answer, I turned the knob. The door opened, and I felt like God's green fool.

Logan was sitting up on his bed with a bath towel draped around his shoulders. The air smelled of cheese and wet wool, and the walls were rancid, but nobody was dead which was certainly a step forward. He nodded at me cordially and blew his nose on a corner of the bath towel; I took a pile of magazines off a stool and sat down. There was an empty bowl and a spoon and a box of crackers on the bed beside him, and I distinctly heard something under the bed make a scratching sound, waiting for crackers and nightfall and bones. Logan's face was gray and thin and he looked older than I remembered. His pencil stubs and his paper and his envelopes were all laid out next to him, and I had bought some postage stamps which I put on top of the careful collection. He covered them over with his hand, and I noticed that it was twitching and full of veins like little blue pipes.

I asked him how he was making out, and for about ten minutes he told me. Somewhere in the story I heard Mrs. Detty's name, and I figured that he must have been sick and that she had come around when I had not. I was so busy sitting there and thinking that I had failed someone again that I missed a couple of sentences. I said "What?" trying to sound very involved and concerned. He repeated patiently, he was trying to win a freezer full of food ("They come every month for a whole year and stock it up for you again") and I would help him fill out the coupon if I liked, would I? He said he had sent me a message asking me to come, but he guessed it hadn't got to me. I had a peculiar wish to moan. Any of those evenings when I had been sitting around massaging my soul, I could have been there, with my red ballpoint pen, filling out his coupon. I accepted it from him remorsefully and asked if Mrs. Detty had been around. He said no, unless she was the cans of soup, and I dropped the subject because she probably was and I felt guilty enough already.

I asked him who the man was across the hall, and Logan shrugged and said he didn't know, adding only "He shoots very high." I felt depressed, remembering that cheerful O-mouth and the tiny music, but I might have guessed why my jungle man was as blank to himself as he was to me, somewhere out there, stoned, extinguished and turning into his own graveyard. Maybe he and the rats had long talks together inside their walls. I wrote "Geo." neatly on the coupon, and then I looked up and said, "How do you want this? Logan? Longan? Lonergan?" He held out his hand and the towel slid off his shoulder. He jerked as if his old-man flesh was an indecency, and I helped him put it back before I gave him the coupon. He sat there for quite a while, holding it close to his eyes and frowning, and finally he said, "That's good the way it is."

"Just G-e-o?" I said.

"With the dot."

I took it back from him and looked at *Geo.*, and for the life of me I couldn't figure out whether he was giving up at last or whether he was entering a new era of hope under a new alias. I fantasized a truck with two men in it, going their rounds with a month's supply of food for a freezer, looking for a spook named Geo., trailed by dirty brats and clean rats, all with a faraway musical score composed by cobras. I put a flourish under "Geo." and handed the coupon back to him. When he folded it carefully and mailed it inside his cracker box, I felt a little sad.

But I stayed quite a while longer, just sitting around and grunting harmoniously when he made a statement and, on the whole, rather enjoying myself. I thought Geo. and I probably had many meaningful things to communicate and that this was as good a way as any. When I left, I promised to come back soon with more postage stamps. He can put them into the cracker box along with the coupon, and, if there is any truth in the gospel according to Father Bailey, Somebody Somewhere will get it all in His mail.

That wasn't why I went around to see Father Bailey afterwards, though. I went because, on my way to where I was going (which I have now forgotten, so enterprising are my days) I ran into my hostile friend, Detective Sloan. He raised a hand in barest recognition, walking flat and heavy like a cop with a mission. I turned to look after him, and he had turned to look after me, so we both laughed but my own laughter was wan. He came back, and I stood on the sidewalk talking to him for about ten minutes and feeling rather built up. I thought I was doing my corporate image a lot of good (I should have known better) until a pair of skinny black kids came by and produced a scatological sound in duet which, though wordless, communicated their estimate of us with exquisite clarity.

Sloan turned around and gave them an impeccable salute, snapping fingers to brow as if they were the Police Commissioner himself. He looked at them very respectfully for just as long as they could stand it. Their eyes goggled, and they punched each other and brayed, and then suddenly they whisked their tails and disappeared like puffs of dust, plainly outmaneuvered. Sloan said placidly, "They're geniuses, ought to be in a sideshow," and then he added, "Talked with Mig lately?" before I could get my balance back.

I said "No" just to be on the safe side. Anyway, it depended on what he meant by *lately*. He said "Oh" as if he couldn't care less, gave me the precise salute he had just given the kids, and walked off. Maybe it's a habit, I thought, or maybe he thinks I belong in a sideshow too.

I think it was at that point that I decided to drop in casually on Father Bailey and see if he had any news of Mig. He was just on his way out, and we headed west in silence. After a couple of blocks, I began to feel puzzled because, out here on the street, he seemed so small, much more of a nonentity, as if the street itself were swallowing him up. Cuts him down to size, I found myself thinking with an odd satisfaction. Because why would I want Father Bailey cut down to size?

Still, the street this morning would have cut anybody down to size. Once in a while it gets this way. It comes on strong. Colors jump at you like that blood-orange fungus in the woods, and you could run a powerhouse on the electricity. Nobody looks at you straight, but nobody shuffles. The hills are full of coyotes and the elephants are standing in doorways and there are moles in the sewer lapping up cheap wine, but nobody's sick, nobody's doped, nobody's hair lies quiet on a quiet skull, and ordinary people like me and Father Bailey shrink into dried peas.

We passed my black giantess with two of her babies. All her babies stay babies until they are five years old, and then she does an incantation over them and, from that time on, they're senior citizens. She's so lovely, she's like a tree. I got a transistor radio for her once, because she said that Welfare wouldn't (which wasn't true) and she never so much as thanked me, but I walked away and I leaped over a mountain. Today she wasn't knowing anybody, her tall head and her tall shoulders and her tall body way up there in the sky.

I said suddenly to Father Bailey, "Do you hear trumpets?" He said no, but then we turned a corner and there was a wild-eyed injun gypsy thumping a leatherskin drum, no rhythm at all, just the goddam sound. His eyes were perfectly normal but they looked crossed, and the drum kept going ungh-ungh-ungh like a patient invalid. The injun gypsy's hands hung loose from their wrists, and you could almost feel the delicate life trickling backwards up into his elbows, into his shoulders, coming out ungh-ungh-ungh in his head.

"It's a drum," Father Bailey said.

I smiled. The street was getting into me and I was beginning to feel clever and loose-jointed myself. I said I didn't mean the drum, I meant trumpets like the ones the black giantess heard. He replied neatly, "Miss Broma," and I said, *"Miss!* For God's sake, she's got a thousand children."

He said that she seemed to like Miss better, and, because I had been calling her Mrs. right along, I got a jealous feeling that it was his street more than mine after all. He pulled a quarter out of his pocket and gave it to the drummer, and the drummer spat on the pavement and put the quarter somewhere inside his huddle of clothes and went on going ungh-ungh-ungh. The Foundation says not to give money out of your own pocket to people on the street; it diminishes them. A less diminished drummer I never saw.

I cleared my throat and observed rather irrelevantly that I had just run into Detective Sloan. Father Bailey, who was walking quickly now as if the drummer had got into his shoes, said the same thing had happened to him. I said, "Quite by accident, I presume." He said he didn't think Detective Sloan did many things accidentally, and although he sounded sad where I had sounded sarcastic, we seemed to be suddenly united in defiance of hunters. What with Father Bailey looking unusually small today and what with his siding with the hare instead of the hounds, I felt a real affection for him and was able to ask, quite easily, if he thought Mig was in any kind of trouble.

He shook his head, not meaning either yes or no. "Detective Sloan seems to be trying to find out something about drugs being watered down and——"

"Cut," I said pedantically. "Talcum powder, chalk, baking soda—Any of your baking soda missing lately?" He didn't answer, and my scintillating wit turned and hurt me. I wanted very badly to tell him that I didn't really think it was funny myself. "It's the dirtiest business there is," I said lamely. "I don't think even Mig—He's stupid, he's vain, he likes money—" I hung up on that one because, when you're stupid and vain and you like money, what happens next? I said heavily, "I don't have any illusions about Mig."

"Maybe you should. Maybe he needs someone to have illusions about him."

I swallowed an obscenity, one letter at a time, because, when I get obscene in front of Father Bailey, the wrong one feels uncomfortable. "Anna's got enough illusions about him to take him to hell and back."

He smiled gently, the way everyone smiles when you mention Anna, and then said "Of course, she knows him better than we do," which was the ultimate putdown of them all.

I said, very tremolo, very vibrato, "She has F-aith," and added, "Also, no doubt, certain physical compensations."

"Like love," he said placidly.

I started to retort that love isn't only physical, but then I stopped because I thought that might be exactly what he wanted me to say. The street still had its hard, staring sheen and I stared back at it as insolently as I could. A garbage can had been knocked over, and the sidewalk ahead of us was wall-to-wall shuck with a little black girl in a nice pink dress squatting over something she had found. Round, sort of. I hoped that it was a rubber ball. If I took it away from her to find out, she would yell and her mother would rise up out of the sidewalk and try to kill me, and there would be a race riot. It was that kind of a day.

On the other hand, I thought I recognized the kid, in which case I knew her mother who is running her dead husband's fruit store and who tried, at one time, to sell me a ticket in the Irish Sweepstakes. Well, she did sell it to me in a way. I paid for it and then I gave it back to her, keeping my Foundation virtue. Maybe she won. Maybe she's a millionaire right now.

I said vaguely, standing and watching the kid, "Did anybody around here ever win the Irish Sweepstakes?"

Father Bailey said "No" and then added, "I would have heard.—Do you think that's a ball she's got, Richard?"

Oh God, he was human too! I said firmly, yes, it was a ball, and just then a meager black and white dog came up and sniffed at the thing in her fingers and shook its head hard and went away. The pink-dressed little girl smiled very secretly, like she had a rainbow in her hand. I accepted the philosophical concept that some things are better left alone.

We walked a block before Father Bailey said, "I have to stop here," and left me standing on the sidewalk in front of a building sick unto death with most of its windows boarded up or broken and one window open on the very top floor. In the Bailey line of business, I told myself brightly, you have to be prepared to climb them golden stairs.

At the time, this seemed witty, which it does not now. I can only conclude that the street really was peculiar today, shimmering there like dead-sea fruit. The stink and the shine have worn off now, along with my wit. Detective Sloan slid a can of maggots into my brain, and I know that I ought to go in search of Mig, but I am afraid of what I will find. I was also afraid to take the thing, whatever it was, from the little girl's hands, and for much the same reason. But the little girl has a home that I know about, and a mother that I have met, and a dead father who was a good man and who used to run a fruit store, and, whatever the thing was in her hands, it is important to remember that she handled it very gently. I have seen small children on these streets stop to pat a junkie lying in a doorway, pat him gravely and tenderly as if he were their very own dog, their very own kitten. They have families, these kids, and they carry their families with them inside their heads so that their lives are a crazy combination of very wild and fierce and very solid and good. Sometimes I forget about their families and I get scared, and then sometimes I remember them so well that I can almost hear them in all the streets, running underground, all the strong roots talking to each other.

But Mig doesn't have any roots, which is why I am afraid.

So here is my brand of no-faith, Father Bailey. If Jeannie was here, I could explain it to her, but that Rose of Tralee is lost for good and all. If Ellyn was here, she would explain it to me, but that thornbush will only scratch me once. If Professor Blount was here, he would tell me that this is the stuff of which great literature is made. No, he wouldn't do that. I don't ever remember his being mean.

Still, I keep wanting to believe that the little girl in pink actually found a rubber ball in the garbage. Strike *actually*— it's bad writing.

I do believe that the little girl in pink found a rubber ball in the garbage. I actually believe it.

Anyway, I tell myself that I do, and that way I can go to sleep.

32

She woke him out of sleep, saying "Mig, Mig" desperately into his ear. He thought she was having a bad dream, and he turned toward her irritably and shook her shoulder to wake her up. She screamed.

He had never heard Anna scream before, and for a moment he was only astonished. Then, when she tried to sit up, only to double over dreadfully, still screaming, he felt the lurch of his own heart and the coldness of his own blood. He said "Stop it!" loudly so as to be heard over her abandon. "Stop it, you hear?"

She stopped, and her silence was more dreadful than her screams. Her eyes had a white look, and it was as if her lips were parched so that only the thinnest sound came out. He had to lean forward.

"Mig. Mig, help me."

He forced his heart down, and he told her angrily that she was all right. "You ate something like you did the other time." He was trembling but that was because the room was cold. He reached for her hands, to hold her so that he could make her listen. "You ate something bad," he said.

She shook her head, shivering, and her eyes got worse, flooding with pain instead of tears.

"Anna! Anna, what's wrong? You done something?" He didn't know what made him ask it that way, some kind of dull foreboding. He wanted to unsay it and to hold back her answer, but when she moaned, he leaned closer and heard something about "Mama Kraus." He could only guess dimly at what she had done, but even that guess was horrible. Obscenities swelled in his throat like vomit, and he spat them out.

Anna's voice was as small as a child's, and she began to repeat, over and over, very carefully, "Somebody to help me, Mig, somebody to help me. Please, Mig, somebody to help me." After a while, "I'm bleeding," the small child voice said, still carefully. Then she said "Mama?" hopefully, and this time she didn't mean Mama Kraus. She lay back on the bed, holding herself very stiff, and as her mouth pinched and her little chin narrowed, her eyes grew bigger and bigger.

"What do you want me to do?" Mig said. "I don't know what to do. What do you want?" She didn't answer him, and he saw suddenly that the one person who always thought of him first was no longer capable of thinking of anything except what was happening to her body. He had a sudden terrible need for Ernie, a need so violent that for a moment it conjured Ernie up and he stood in the doorway, but then he vanished and there was no one in the room except Mig and this girl who could no longer help Mig.

"Mama?" she said again.

His mind scratched for information like a rat. All the people in the building took care not to know each other, there was not one who would help him. Anyway, what he needed was a doctor. He didn't know any doctors, but he did know where the hospital was, and it bloomed suddenly in his mind. If he could just get Anna to the hospital, he could leave her there, safe in a white bed with people around her. Maybe he would never have to see her again. The way she was now, he almost hated her, and the thought of getting her to that white hospital bed released him. He got up suddenly—too suddenly. He jarred the thin mattress, and she screamed.

He shook his head against the sound and began to dress as fast as he could, pulling on the only jacket that he owned, the fancy shoes that he had been so proud of. She was spoiling everything, he thought angrily, even the shoes didn't look like anything much.

When he asked her if she could stand up, she shook her head, tinily as if even that small movement hurt. He pulled the blanket off her and then he put it back quickly, pretending he had not seen the blood and telling himself that she needed the blanket to keep her warm. It seemed urgent to keep her warm. She was perfectly quiet. She breathed as if she was counting every breath she drew, and perhaps that was what was keeping her so quiet. Once, she moaned. That was when he straightened suddenly, pulling her up into his arms. He was almost surprised to find how easily he could lift her, nothing but the little bones and that careful breathing.

The hospital was ten blocks away. He counted them in his head to make certain. He could not carry her ten blocks, but he could not stay here either. She would start to scream again and maybe go on screaming until she stopped screaming forever. He said miserably, "Can you get your arm around my neck?"

She did it somehow. He could feel the cupped palm against his hair like a little bug or something it was so light. He said out loud, "Don't die, Anna." Then he sighed deeply and began his journey.

The stairs were not as bad as he had thought they would be, because they were so narrow that the walls acted as support. He slid between them like a snake, holding her under her arms and knees, half across his shoulder, breathing in-out-in-out in time to her breathing. Once in a while she made a little clucking sound in her throat, but mostly she just breathed. He managed the door without having to put her down, which was a small triumph. The night air striking against his face felt so good that for a moment he thought, with sudden innocent hope, it might revive her altogether.

He stood holding her and looking up and down the street— Ernie? Mrs. Detty? an unlikely Sanitation truck on the garbage-choked road? anybody to help him get to the hospital. The street was as quiet as cats. Someone was slumped in a doorway of the boarded-up junkhouse across the street, but his or her body was nothing more than a heap of itself. A long way off, a police siren screamed softly like Anna had screamed.

She was getting heavier. Maybe she was dead already. He held her tighter, and she made a small sound. Not dead.

He stepped out into the road. There were headlights two blocks down—probably a gypsy cab crawling along down the street and not so far off. He willed it to come toward him, and it did.

What he had to do now was get into the middle of the road and wave his arms, but he couldn't do that holding Anna. He laid her down in the gutter as gently as he could, and she gave that strange little cluck and sagged against the curb. He couldn't look at her or even think about her because he had to get the cab to stop, and he went straight to the middle of the street, yelling and waving. He got there just in time to see the headlights turn off, one block away, and vanish into nothing.

Once more there was only Mig and Anna and the night. He had no idea what to do now that the cab was lost to him— whether to stay with her or to go somewhere (where?) and try to find somebody (who?). He went back to the curb and, kneeling beside her, he touched her shoulder and asked her what he should do.

The little rag body fell against him, and once again he thought he was going to die of fear. He went down on his knees and put his arms around her and said "Anna," and she answered him indistinctly but, somewhere inside the blurred words, he heard his own name. It had, at least, the effect of making him feel that he existed.

Doggedly, he propped her up. He left once more and went to stand in the street, looking up and down it and praying in a rage for some kind of miracle to happen, for Anna's Jesus Mary and Joseph to be of some use. When he finally did see a pair of headlights again, he got the idea that it was a police car, prowling silently, ready to put out a quick paw. He was afraid of trouble, but he was more afraid that Anna was dying. The car kept coming toward him, and he threw up his hands and shouted.

The brakes screamed. Everything screamed tonight. It wasn't a police car, after all, just a car with a man inside it. The man's face was greasy-white through the windshield, and he had taken both hands off the wheel and was waving them like some crazy kind of a hex dance, scared silent and shrieking inside.

Mig lunged for the car door and wrenched it open, almost falling backwards because he had been so sure it would be locked. Any gull who didn't know enough to lock his doors at this hour of the night, in these streets, was inviting a sudden end. Mig, in his own territory, felt a swift and fierce advantage and, when the man reached to grab the door back, Mig fought him for it and won. They stared at each other, the man's face close because he was sprawled across the seat.

"My girl's sick," Mig said between his teeth.

"Aaa-aah." It was not yes or no, just a cry to be let loose of.

"You take us to the hospital." He repeated it. "Take us to the hospital."

"Aaaaa." Like his tongue had caught in his throat. "Give me the door, it's my car, get away from me. Get away from me, it's my car."

The word "car" spoke in Mig's head. He did what Ernie would have done, because Ernie liked cars and talked about them all the time. Once, he had showed Mig how easy it was to slip a car away from the curb if its dumb owner had been as stupid as dumb owners usually were and left the key in the lock. It was the key that gave the power.

Mig snatched for the key, turned it and pulled it out. He felt almost merry for one wild moment, and if Anna hadn't been lying against the curb, he might have pushed the man onto the street and taken the car for his own, splendidly crazy and dazzled with speed, howling and powerful. Only, he had no idea how to drive. He would have wished for Ernie again, except that now he held the key in his hand and the fool who owned the car was a shivering sack of nothing.

Holding the key tight, Mig went back to the gutter and took his girl out of it. She lay against him, and he lugged her over and pushed her into the front seat next to the man, and then he pushed in beside her and pulled the door shut. "I know where the hospital is," he said, put the key into its lock, and sat back.

The man stayed huddled in the corner, his hands between his knees and his eyes swiveled away as if he would catch a plague if he so much as looked at Anna. "I won't take her," he said. "She'll die in my car."

Mig said very simply, *"You'll* die in your car if you don't," and his hands sketched a stabbing in the air. He wished there was a knife in them, but he was the smart one who never carried a knife. The man just looked at him, and after a moment he leaned over and turned the key.

That was all. The man wouldn't drive right up to the hospital door, but it was close enough. Mig got out of the car and pulled Anna after him. She was absolutely still, terribly light, but maybe that was because he was getting used to carrying her. He shifted her against him, and the man clawed at the handle and slammed the door shut so hard that he nearly knocked them both off balance. The tires screeched getting away, the little man and his car both safe together.

Mig said to Anna, "Put your arm around my neck," but this time she didn't do it. He couldn't get a good hold on her and she kept slipping, but he thought of the safe white bed that was so near now and he managed to put one foot in front of the other and to hang on.

He carried her as far as the glass door. There were lights behind it, and people coming and going, and suddenly, reaching out from everywhere, there were a great many hands.

33

My mother done told me I should never sit up until three o'clock in the morning. But this is unique. I am creating a five-thumb exercise.

A man down the block is yapping like a dog, or a dog down the block is yapping like a man. I have been lying awake, groaning with sympathy for my sleepless self, and the moon coming in now is light enough to type by. There is one good thing about my stately old-world lodgings, I can type whenever I want to—not because the walls are thick (they are made of potato parings) but because we are accustomed to aggressive noise, twenty-four hours a day. My skilled ears have learned to listen, all at the same time, to a police siren ripping the street, to the man next door clearing his throat like a crow (awk-hawk-caw-hawk), to my dripping faucet, to a sobbing baby (they sob to attract attention; if they yell, no one hears them), and to a Negro voice and a Spanish voice calling each other vile but elegant epithets just under my window. My own delicately tapping typewriter, five thumbs working as one, is underscored by my hawking neighbor's radio. He leaves it on all night, turned very high, so that it can sing and speak and assure him that he is still authentically alive.

If Jeannie was here, or Ellyn, or Carol or Virginia or Miranda (whoever they were) or the witch that Codd was seducing at the bar, or someone comforting (like, say, a teddy-bear?), I might be able to go back to sleep. But it is now almost three-thirty, and the moon if it ever really existed has gone behind a cloud. I threw in that bit about typing by moonlight because it sounded effective, although Professor Blount once told me gravely that I would go straight to hell if I insisted on striving for effect, and no one ever spoke a truer word. I am typing by my gooseneck lamp, sitting in a pool of electric light and looking, I fancy, very like Herman Melville.

There is a line of Melville's—"Of all the tools used in the shadow of the moon, men are most apt to get out of order." I wish that I had been the man who wrote *Moby Dick,* but let us admit that, if I had been, I would have used that line as the opening whereas Melville threw it in casually about halfway through. If I had Melville here, I would slit his throat.

The first line of my own novel was, "He lived inside a bubble." I still think it was good. There was nothing wrong with my novel, in fact, except the 94,000 words that came after the first line. That's why Melville put his line into the middle of his book—a brilliant literary device . . . . Like I should go back to writing short stories, Mr. Melville, instead of exercises under a gooseneck lamp? Since, as you have taken the trouble to point out, sir, men are the tools most apt to get out of order. I am out of order, Mig is out of order, would to God that my neighbor's radio were out of order. (Does this mean that I am not as immune to sound as I thought? a sign of life moving in my old ruins?)

I am on the dangerous side of asking myself what I am doing here. A dawn question, tiresome and romantic. What I should be doing is to write a sensitive short story about two old characters I had to go and see this afternoon. They are two little black people (ah, bwana! like the little brown brothers of the British Empire—but they *are* little, and they *are* black, and what am I supposed to do about it?) Two little black people, repeat this resolutely, who have lived for thirty of the fifty years of their married life in the same building on the same street. Their building was once neat and respectable. It is now peopled with junkies and hopheads and grifters and children and Afro-browed revolutionaries, and fathers and mothers and rats and thieves. Also a silent, diligent man known as Shutters who runs a numbers operation as if it were a church festival and who has been in jail at least seven times for a habit of using his knife on the opposition. My old black couple lives outside and beyond all this. They are so patient, so durable and so humble that my skin crawls with exasperation whenever I have to visit them and I spend the next twenty-four hours feeling ashamed of myself.

I know why my skin crawls. It is because they remind me of my Aunt Dorothy, who was also patient, durable and humble. She was actually a cousin of my father's. I was supposed to call her Auntie because she was lonely (my fault?) and she always embraced me until I squirmed. These two old black people embrace me with their pathetic eyes, and I come away with my heart aching, a profound sense of terrible guilt, and an avid delight in escaping to the wild, impenitent street. The old man follows me to the door, for the last word, and it is always the same last word, and I stand there, waiting for it helplessly, my head bent like a good priest or a rabbi or a social worker or anyone who can't get away. What he wants to tell me each time is that he knows his wife will pass (he never says "die") before he does. "God wants her," he says with a sort of stubborn despair, "and you can't blame Him." He holds onto my sleeve tightly as if I could do something to postpone God's plans, and I murmur responses. Tears well in his eyes, I feel sympathetic itchings in my own. Before we both fall into bathos, I have fled, Aunt Dorothy winging behind me.

Quaint people. I must put them in a book some day, and then I will not have to think about them any more.

Mrs. Detty was telling me last week about a man who used to live in the same building. She was lecturing me on how you can never tell about people, and she used this man as an example. He lived one floor up from my sentimental old black horrors, and he was a sentimental old white horror not to be believed. He worked as a bill collector of a loan agency, and for an entire year he managed to produce a perfect collection record. It turned out that the secret of his phenomenal success was that he had a heart like thick custard and he was paying all the uncollectable bills himself. When he went broke, as was rather inevitable, he disappeared completely, and it is believed that he left the United States and is living in a place called Kansas.

If I get her message correctly, Mrs. Detty is trying to prepare me for the possibility that my gentle old blacks are members in good standing of the local Mafia. It may be so. Mrs. Detty never disappoints me.

Well, my soul is getting peaceful and my body is getting sleepy. The yapping mandog has fallen silent, the baby sobs no more. Even my neighbor's radio is turned low, rocking its rock to sleep, its commercials muffled. I feel myself growing tender and very wise. I can no longer remember what it was that made me so wakeful. Mig, probably. I make a rosary of that poor kid and count him religiously on my fingers. There can be a dozen reasons why he hasn't been around recently. If Anna was sick, I would be the first one he would come to. Thin comfort—but that's what I'm here for, isn't it?

(Exit, laughing.) Thin Comfort lies on his thin mattress and pulls up his thin blanket, as the lights slowly dim.

34

They had taken her away from him and had left him there in the hospital lobby, sitting on a black leather chair at four in the morning.

There were others waiting like him, gray-faced, dawn-weary, bone-scared. A fat girl had fallen asleep, her legs spread and a baby spread across them, her mouth sagging open. Opposite, a rusty old man kept looking at her furtively, his own mouth shut tight and prim but his eyes wide and greedy. Two middle-aged women sat on a bench, holding hands, or at least one of them was trying to and the other kept pulling away. The first one had a box of Kleenex and a bad cold.

After a bit, Mig stopped looking at any of them and watched the man at the information desk, who was small and had narrow, neat hands and who seemed to have been answering people's questions all his life.

When a young man in white came into the lobby and looked around quickly, Mig stood up, thinking he was the one who was being looked for, but the very cool look went right over him and the tiny gesture of *come* was for the two women on the bench. They got up at once, and this time the one with the cold let her hand be held. Mig tried to pretend that he had known he was not the one who was wanted and that he had only intended to get a magazine from the table. He selected one and strolled back very casually to his chair, but no one was watching him anyway. The fat girl slept, the old man slavered.

The second hand on the moon of the electric clock swept around and around, and the minutes followed it, piling up time. He began to wonder if anyone at all knew he was here, and he tried to think backwards painstakingly. They had taken Anna away from him. They had asked him his name: Mig. When they asked his last name, he had shrugged and, after a moment, they hadn't cared that much. They asked him what had happened, and he had said that he did not know and was almost able to convince himself that this was the truth. They asked him where he lived, and he shrugged again. They seemed perfectly used to this kind of answer and not unfriendly, and so, when they told him to wait on the chair in the lobby, he had waited on the chair in the lobby.

But that was hours ago, and no one had come to ask more questions or even to yell at him to go away, and he thought he might as well get up, in a minute or two, and walk through the glass door and walk back to his room. Anna would not be there, of course. Anna would be here. She was certainly all right, in a good white bed. All he had to do was walk outside and go home and sleep and come back in the morning . . . . .

She was certainly all right.

But he stayed. He leafed through the magazine, large, shiny, full of photographs, things happening to people in places he had never even heard of. He read what little he could, setting his teeth in anger against the many words he did not know. After a while, the old man stopped staring at the girl and fell asleep, his head dropping. The old chin looked like melted tallow. He breathed like Anna had breathed, as if he didn't have much air left and was trying to save it. Mig drifted back to the magazine. The ads were the best part, and twice he found his beautiful American girl, always with a beautiful

American man. He began to imagine in his head that this was his girl and that he could do with her whatever he wanted to do, but his dream went in tired circles and was disappointing.

He looked at the clock again. The second hand which had swept with such speed was now slowing, and it ticked in absolute silence, promising nothing. In ten minutes, it would be the hour, and then he would get up and go. But, when it came to the hour, he was still there.

Finally, he slept—lightly and without any dreams at all. When someone shook his shoulder, he woke in absolute clearness, knowing exactly where he was. The black leather chair was his bed and his home. The man shaking his shoulder was another man in white, not the one who had come into the lobby before. This one was older, plainly a doctor. Mig looked up at him with that peculiar mixture of docility and alertness which had always won him so much from Mr. Harris, although at this moment he did not know precisely what he was trying to win.

The doctor said, "Your name's Mig," a statement, not a question. "No last name? Just Mig?" Mig looked into a corner of the lobby and said that Mig was what they called him. "No last name to Anna either?" said the doctor, and Mig shrugged.

"Has she got a family?"

Mig thought of Anna's mother, and then he lied and said "No."

"Who brought her here?"

He could answer that, and he said eagerly, "I brought her," because he was certain that bringing a person to a hospital was a safe and right thing to have done.

The doctor looked at him without expression, and then said, "Brought her here in more ways than one, I should think. You know what happened?"

If he had said no right away, it might have been possible to hide from himself forever, but all he answered with was silence. The doctor gave a short, rather angry laugh. "Do you know what she did? Do you know where she went?"

He knew. He knew it in a half-twilight place of his mind, remembering that Mama whose name she had said before she called on her own Mama. He moved his body a little, as if he could not quite tolerate the doctor's eyes. The doctor said again, "Do you know where she went?"

"I didn't tell her to go," Mig said sullenly. "I didn't tell her to do anything."

"Cautious little rat," the doctor said, very cleanly, as if he was talking about someone else entirely.

Mig defended himself. "I brought her here."

"So she wouldn't die in your bed?"

"No!" He said it explosively, because he could easily have left her to die in the street, and he had not done that, he had brought her here. And then the word got through to him, and he said "She's dead" as if he had always known how it would be and as if, by saying it quickly himself, he need not hear it from the doctor.

"No, she's not dead, but it's no fault of yours." The doctor paused, and then he said, heavily and cruelly, "I'd like the name of your butcher."

The words meant nothing to Mig at all, they might have been in another language. He looked at the doctor so dumbly that some of the terrible ignorance, the vast non-knowledge, the arrogant stupidity of everything that had happened must have spoken for him. The doctor said "Oh God" but not as a prayer, and then he said wearily, "You sure she doesn't have a family?"

This time he didn't lie, but mostly because he didn't think his lies were being believed. He avoided the question with a vague gesture and said, "Someone will take her." Someone

185

would have to take her, and there were many agencies called Welfare. For himself, he wished only to turn around and walk away and never come back. Never see this man or Anna again.

"No family at all," said the doctor, accepting it. "Well, rejoice. You don't have a family either. There won't be any baby."

The gates of Hell opened a little, and Mig's mind leaped to shut them. "It wasn't my baby," he said. "It wasn't mine."

"Well, God damn you, my little man," the doctor said, very carefully, very pleasantly. "And just whose baby was it then?"

Mig shut his eyes. "Mine."

They were both silent, and then the doctor said, "Come back around noon, Mig. Maybe you can see her then." He sounded very tired. "She should have come to us earlier, you know, we could have taken care of her.—You didn't know, did you?"

Mig shook his head.

"You don't know anything. Well—" The doctor looked at him for a moment, then shrugged and walked away.

Mig stood there, hating him, hating his doctor-smugness and his power and his long, clean hands. He acted like he owned the place and maybe he did, but, if Anna died, it would be his fault and he wouldn't look so big. He was probably a clumsy ape, anyway. It was a kind of pleasure to imagine the doctor, failing miserably, crawling to him in failure, sodden with failure, and he played with the idea until Anna pushed her soft way into his mind and he thought of her as being dead. He rejected the thought wildly.

But maybe she *was* dead. Maybe the doctor's questions were a trap, trying to make him out a murderer. Maybe he would hang?

He knew better. He stood in the hospital lobby, and he knew perfectly well that this hospital was not a trap. What they could do for Anna, they would do, and he assured himself—anxiously, superstitiously—that he was not really angry with the doctor. He needed the doctor's help.

He looked at the clock on the wall. The time between now and noon was the same as forever. He was hungry and he was tired, and Anna was not here to comfort him. He thrust his hands deep into his pockets and walked out quickly, past the information desk and through the glass doors, trying to look independent, trying desperately to look as if he knew exactly where he was going.

35

I woke this morning, full of good resolutions. I got out of bed, feeling capable and intelligent, precisely the kind of man I would hire if I were a Foundation. My clear brain rejected all my uneasiness about Mig. I even saw his avoidance of me as a sign of that budding self-reliance which I, Foundation gardener, am supposed to tend with zeal.

My composure was so inclusive that the street around me reflected it. The garbage seemed neat. The lamp posts stood erect. The fire hydrants were of a keen, responsible nature. A shambling junkie, wearing a string necktie, was a sign of civilization returning to our shores, and the heads of small children looked lively and brave.

I went first, and with total confidence, to Mrs. Detty, tracing her mouse-tracks until I found her coming out of one of those caves that the Law calls tenements and talking loudly to herself. She acknowledged me curtly and swept me into the current of her stream of words. It was a very bitter stream. She was using vocabulary unbecoming to a social worker, phrases she does not approve when I use them, but I could not harass her with teasing just then. Her mind was directed dagger-like against those lords of the slums who live "outside the city" and who have bifurcated names for their corporate identity like Fran-Jo or Fast-Buck or God-Save. After a while, she ran down like a clock and we walked in silence. I knew she was paying me a compliment by letting me join her torrent and then share her quiet.

When a grubby coffee-satin baby toddled into the gutter and sat down deliberately in wet slop, Mrs. Detty rewound. She dredged it out and handed it, dripping, to me. Obedience itself, I held the object over my shoulder, while she mopped its rear severely with the combination dishcloth-and-banner that she carries in her large black handbag. I loved Mrs. Detty even more than usual at that moment, but I did not love the baby. Although it smelled interestingly of slops and cooking fat, it had sticky fingers that paddled on my neck and tiny steel-wool braids that scratched at my ear. "I do not believe," said Mrs. Detty unemotionally, "that I can keep anything clean," and I knew that this quite unnecessary and sentimental tableau was only her way of putting her morning hate to some good purpose. When I set the baby down, it went straight back into the gutter as if it were a cockroach. Mrs. Detty put her cloth back into her handbag and thanked me for my help.

We picked up our silence and marched another block before she suddenly announced that I would make a good father. I blushed. (There is a tendency in my generation to blush when accused of being in any way respectable.) I responded with a dignity which was wasted on her, because she had observed my embarrassment. It quite cheered her up, and she made that peculiar little ticking sound which, with her, is a giggle. She and Jeannie used to tick together, sometimes at my expense. I thought therefore of Jeannie and I thought of being a father (any kind, not necessarily a good one) and from there I went to Anna, who is so visibly motherless and fatherless. I said hastily, extracting myself from Mrs. Detty's funhouse, "Have you seen Mig lately?"

"There's nothing wrong with being a good father," she answered.

I said snappishly that this was true. Had she seen Mig lately?

She said no and then announced that I shouldn't put all my eggs into one basket, a remark which made me really angry. I said under my breath, impolitely, that it was none of her business, but she only shrugged back, opposing her unruffled biddy hen to my arrogant young cock. "He's been hanging around Mrs. Peters," she said, and added, "Poor soul," not meaning Mig.

So, all right. I know he hangs around Mrs. Peters. I have heard her speak of him as her "dear boy," which nauseates me. She is awash with every kind of slop. Poor soul, indeed.

Since Mrs. Detty had no news of Mig for me, I left her at the next stop and went off to hunt up Ernie, who might be able to answer some of those questions that I was so unwilling to ask. Looking for him, I came upon Geo. Lonergan-Logan, teetering venturesomely down the middle of the sidewalk. He was holding up exceedingly well until he saw me, and then he clawed at my shoulders with his skinny hands and gasped like a fish. "You're doing fine," I assured him. "The last time I saw you, you were dying." I was charmed to see so clearly through his fraudulence, and he was equally charmed to find himself so transparent. He made a noise that sounded dismayingly like hee-hee and asked me to take him home because he had walked too far. I turned him in the right direction and let him sag elaborately on my supporting arm. We made a very big thing of it, bright youth and hoary age.

There was not a dry eye on the block, and a passing postman saluted us out of sheer gratitude. This is a bad time of the month for postmen, with Welfare and Social-Security checks arriving in the mail and kooks and thugs and juggers hanging around and plotting to snatch them. I think that Geo. and I made his day a little brighter.

We lurched on, Geo. getting heavier and more senile by the minute and me regretting my good impulses. I got him up his stairs by prodding his rear and, when we reached his landing, I was more winded than he was. He said he had brought me here (brought me!) because he had something for me to see, and it was true, he did. It was a letter announcing that he had won a tiepin engraved with his own initials and that he would receive the tiepin just as soon as he mailed in his order for a magnetic compass, to be attached to the dashboard of his car, at the unbelievable price of $2.95. He showed me the coupon, and then he closed the slits of his old eyes and rocked his old head and said to me, very wistfully, that he didn't suppose I needed a magnetic compass for my car, did I? I was about to say no, but there was something in his face that shook me with grief. No sense to it, really—he was not only perfectly happy at that moment but even rather tough and shrewd. I heard myself saying, sure, sure, nothing I wanted more than a magnetic compass. I could always get the car later.

I filled out the coupon for him, including the message about "G.L." to be engraved on the tiepin, and I did it very carefully because I had decided to present the compass to Codd, telling him that it was a gift from an old admirer of his in the heart of the ghetto. If that outlay of funds by a poverty-stricken wretch did not shake up Codd's sensibilities, nothing ever would. He need not know that the poverty-stricken wretch was me.

I said to Geo., as I shaped his initials exquisitely with my red pen, that I certainly appreciated his letting me in on the ground floor in this magnetic-compass deal. He said I was welcome. When we parted, we parted as friends, he richer by one initialled tiepin and me poorer by two dollars and ninety-five cents.

On the stairs, I met the Ruiz's oldest boy who told me hurriedly that his mother was going to get married or have triplets or enter a convent or something of that sort. I responded with vague but hearty good wishes. The boy is eighteen years old, married, and living at home with a bosomy girl who is not his wife. I pride myself on a rather good grasp of the local family trees.

I went on down the stairs, beginning to feel easier about Mig again. The day was developing so loose-jointed that I was ready to imagine a hundred acceptable reasons for not having seen him lately. Outside, without even looking for him, I found Ernie, and the first question Ernie asked was, Had I seen Mig? I said no, and added that he was probably at home with Anna. Ernie said he had just come from there and that there wasn't no one, larding even that small and messy sentence with his little nuggets of verbal smut, which always seem to me peculiarly sad because he obviously rejoices in them. In a better world, Ernie would have been a master philologist, but, as it is, he has trouble spelling his own name.

"Maybe Lou knows," he said, and then he gave me a sudden, frightened, sideways look and ran away, swiftly and silently, as if he had said too much. I almost ran after him, but I didn't. If you start running after someone here, some joker at an upstairs window may just take a potshot at you, not caring whether he hits hare or hound, just feeling itchy. There is more than one reason why us rabbits in these parts sometimes act lethargic.

Thanks to Ernie, all my easiness was gone again. I went to find Father Bailey, and for once he was home. He let me in through his unbolted door (I wish to God he would bolt it) and he looked at me with mild astonishment. It was Ernie who had so disheveled my tranquil brow. Up to Ernie, it had been a pretty good day.

I sat down on the chair and, the moment I sat, I knew that I wasn't going to tell him anything at all. If I once started to talk, I would say too much. Mrs. Detty was right about my putting all my eggs into one basket. I think she knows at the back of that knotty little head of hers that I use Mig like one of those magnetic compasses I am buying from Geo. I steer my-self by Mig. If I can pull Mig out of the quicksand of his life here, I can pull myself out of my own quicksand. Call it a wager.

The truth is that I cannot stand two failures—my book, about which I can be quite funny and rueful, and now Mig, about whom I can be neither. I don't know why I feel so sure that something has gone wrong with Mig and that, very soon now, I am going to learn what it is. But I am sure. And when I know, I think I may not want to stay here any more, not among all these people who seem to want to be my strangers.

Father Bailey was looking at me, and he said, "Richard." And I said "Yes?" and he said, "It will be all right, Richard." I stood up, and I said carefully, "Excuse me, but I don't think it will be all right," and then I said "Excuse me" again and walked out.

I am back at my typewriter now. My wager is still on. The odds may even be in my favor. I may find out tomorrow that Mig—my compass, my touchstone—continues to serve me well.

I *will* find out tomorrow. I have raised my fist to shake it at the ceiling. It mocks me, a monstrous shadow fist answering back, and I feel jaunty for a moment and worldly-wise and amused by Life which hangs over me with that inevitable capital L.

Cool it till tomorrow, Old Boy. All will be well.

36

He had not gone home that night at all. The streets were his home.

He could not make plans, because there was nothing to plan for. If he could find Ernie, Ernie would do anything for him, but there was nothing really that he wanted done. When he leaned his head against a wall, he felt vaguely dizzy, and he stood still, searching his mind, like going through empty pockets but not finding anything. After a while, he let his body sag, let it find the sidewalk, let it rest. He fell heavily asleep, one arm thrown out, touching the wall for reassurance.

When he woke, wretched and cold, there was enough light to make the street lamp look pale, and he was surprised to find that the wall was part of the hospital and that he had not really left it at all. He felt as if flies were crawling over him, and his very bones were dry. He put his hands over his eyes, and his fingers jerked. He had an obsessive desire for water, not to drink but to wash in, and he terribly wanted to know what time it was but could not remember why he wanted to know.

He walked back into the hospital, feeling old, and when he looked at the clock he remembered why he wanted to know the time. The doctor had said he could see Anna at noon. The hours between now and then stretched into forever. He chose a corridor to go down, and it was the wrong one. A woman stared at him, and he turned and went in the opposite direction until he found the door that said *Men*. It was not locked, which surprised him a little; if it had been locked, he would have beat on its panels. He went into the blind impersonal whiteness of tile and leaned over the nearest washbowl, retching dryly and without result. He turned the faucet on with a kind of ritual care and let the bowl fill with water. When he plunged his hands in, soaking the cuffs of his jacket, he could feel coolness moving all through him. The sight of his own face in the mirror reminded him that, here at least, there was one person he knew.

When he went back to the lobby, he was not cleaner, but the wet cuffs gave him a point of sensation on which he could concentrate. The chair was empty again, and he sat down on it and began to rock his body back and forth. He rocked endlessly, lullingly for a while, and then he stopped and put his elbows on his knees and sat staring at the gray floor. It had pink marbled streaks in it. He thought that maybe Anna was dead, in spite of what the doctor had told him. Maybe they had taken her away already and she was laid out in some funeral parlor with flowers around her. He had been to a funeral once (a boy he knew had fallen off a roof, sniffing glue, it had been a mistake to go to the funeral) and there had been a lot of flowers. Fear snuffled at him like a cat.

A black man with a mop said, "Lift your feet, boy." He didn't like being called "boy," but it was a perfectly gentle voice. He stood up, pretending he had been planning to move anyway, and went over to the desk. There was a woman at it now, instead of a man, not very young, with a flat pink face. He straightened his jacket and hid his wet cuffs, but he was in trouble right from the start because Anna had come here without any last name. By the time the woman had thought to look under A for Anna, she was openly annoyed. He felt pale and scrawny and when he said, "I want to see her," he sounded belligerent when he most wanted to be persuasive.

She shook her head. "Not now. She's not on Critical, you know."

Always they were saying "you know" to him when he did not know. He had no idea what "critical" meant, and so he feared the word automatically. She must have seen his ignorance, because after a moment she told him that it meant he would have to wait for Visiting Hours.

If she was still under A for Anna and could be visited, she was not dead. He said, "When's that?" and, when she told him, he told her he could not wait that long, the doctor had promised noon. He said it hopelessly because he did not know the doctor's name.

She was looking at him, however, instead of just listening, and she said, "Have you been here all night?" He nodded, and her flat face looked a little more alive. "Come back around ten-thirty," she told him. "I'll see what I can do. And get yourself something to eat before you fall on your face."

He looked once more at the clock on the wall, memorizing it, and then he walked out of the hospital without thanking her, but he was not ungrateful, only confused. He could not go back to his room; in fact, he would not. He found a sandwich shop open, but he had exactly twenty cents in his pocket. Anyway, he didn't feel like eating. He asked for a mug of coffee with milk in it, and then he added as much sugar as he could get away with under the counter man's watchful eye. The coffee cleared his head a little, and he knew what he wanted to do. He wanted to find Ernie.

But somewhere in the black streets, Ernie had vanished. While Mig hunted, he could feel a small cold spot spreading in his heart, and the self that he had found briefly in the men's room mirror turned into a stranger again. He felt lonely and his head was full of echoes, and, after a while, he simply gave up and went back to the hospital.

The woman was still at the desk, but she was busy with a sallow-faced man and two whining children, and her eyes went right past him. Anyway, it was not nearly ten-thirty. He found another magazine to hold and went back to the black leather chair which he was now beginning to think of as his, and he sat down to wait. Inside him was a fist of fear. He just wanted everything to be all over, all the feeling. He just wanted to go to sleep and to wake up somewhere else with nobody expecting him to do anything.

He got part of his wish. The lobby was warm, and sleep covered him like fog. He fought it vaguely, believing he ought to stay awake, but it crept up from the floor, lapped at his feet, pressed against his thighs, closed his eyelids and smothered his face.

When he woke, the clock told him that he was fifteen minutes late. He stood up too suddenly and fell back against the chair arm, where he stayed for a moment before he shook himself like a dog and walked across the lobby to the desk.

This time she knew him, and she raised her hand in a peremptory gesture that he had seen a thousand times in his short life. It was the gesture of the person in power. He was afraid to say anything, because he supposed that she could keep him from seeing Anna if she wanted to. He kept his head down and his angry eyes hidden, waiting while she used the card file at her elbow, the telephone in her neat white hands, the notepad under her fingers. When she wrote something on a piece of paper and handed it to him, he realized that she had not been neglecting him at all. "You can go up now," she said. "Back ward, fourth floor. Give them this."

He took the paper and mumbled something, and she misunderstood him and told him where the elevator was, which was in plain sight. He got into it, along with two men and a woman, all in white coats, and, when one of them looked at him, he said "Fourth floor?" as if it was a question and not a request. When he got out, he was on the fourth floor but it took trial and error and a piling-up of maddening stupidities before he found the right ward. A stout woman accepted his piece of paper.

Halfway down the long room, he saw Anna. She was among

the sick, the dying and, for all he knew, the dead. She was among yellow faces and gray faces and black faces, and she was even smaller than he remembered. She was unbelievably small under the white sheet—the clean white sheet that he had pictured for her so passionately—and her face was very pale and shut away. He touched her hand, but she did not open her eyes. The stout woman said from behind his shoulder (she must have followed him, why had she followed him? he was instantly fearful), "She's been sleeping," and then she added, "She keeps asking for Joseph. Are you Joseph?"

Mig, born Joseph, denied his birthright instantly. The woman shrugged and said that maybe Joseph, whoever he was, would come later. A passion of real jealousy shook Mig, and he said very quickly, "I don't mean I'm not Joseph, it's what I was born." He was afraid now that he would not be believed, having denied it. "She's the only one that calls me that. I *forgot*," he said.

She looked at him with diminished interest, said "Let her come awake by herself," and left.

He could not wait. He touched Anna's hand again, and her eyes flew open. He felt for a moment as if a net had been thrown over his head, and he wanted to run. If she called him Joseph now, he would go away and never come back.

But she said "Mig," and his hand stayed on hers. He leaned over and said clearly, "You're all right, Anna, they're taking good care of you." She said something about "Mama" and, without thinking, he said, "Mama Kraus?" When she looked sick and moved her head no, he wished he had not spoken the name. He had only done it because he was afraid of the other Mama too. If Anna's Mama had wanted to kill him before, when her daughter left home, she would much more want to kill him now, when she learned what he had done.

It was the first time Mig had really admitted to himself just what it was he had done. From habit and from fear, he turned his guilt into a weapon. He said, "You shouldn't have gone to

Mama Kraus. You should have told me. I would have helped you." She stayed silent, and after a while he said defensively, "Well, I didn't know."

She let him have his lie. Nothing seemed to matter very much to her, and her eyes had closed again. He felt that cramping fist of fear, and he put the palm of his hand uncertainly against her cheek. "Anna?"

She answered him with her small voice, not opening her eyes. "Mig. Take me home with you."

"You're too sick."

"I'll be well. I want to go home."

"You can't now. You're too sick. You might have died."

"*Sì,*" said the little Italian girl she had been. After a minute, she added, very slowly, "Can I see Mama?"

"Anna. No."

She was silent again, and he thought that he had won, but then the tears began to come slowly from her closed eyes and to gather against her thin, pale cheeks. Her body lay there crying, while the rest of her seemed to be slipping away from him. His terror was sudden and absolute, and he was jolted into a promise. "I'll get your mother, Anna. I'll find her and bring her here." He would not think ahead. All he wanted was for her to stop crying. "It will be all right," he said, and then he committed himself, recklessly. "I'll tell her we're married—Anna! I'll buy you a ring."

Her eyes flew open then, and she gave him a look of such love that he nearly drowned. She turned her head on the pillow and put her lips against his wrist, and he jerked away as if she had burned him. He did not know what to do. He looked around, but no one was watching. At least, she was not crying any longer, which he could not stand. He stood up, and she made a frail movement with her hand, trying to keep him. "They won't let me stay," he said, wishing that a nurse would appear and make it true.

Anna's eyes would not let him go, and, to keep from having

to see them, he leaned down and laid his cheek against hers. Her body and his own memory trapped him, and when her thin arms went up around his neck, he did not pull away. Behind him, a voice said sharply, "Be careful!"

He unclasped Anna's hands and held the scant flesh and the little bones just long enough to ease her down on the bed, but somehow she still clung. He knew what she was waiting to hear, and so he said it. "I'll be back, Anna. I'll be back for the Visiting Hours." And then she let him go, and he left her to the nurse.

He was outside on the street and two blocks away before he realized what he had done. He heard himself say out loud, "Like I was crazy or something!" and it was true. In his right mind, he would never have made those promises to Anna, he who had always kept her so casually in her right, convenient place. Bring her mother to the hospital? Buy her a ring, take her on as if he belonged to her, as if they were married? He'd see her dead first.

Oh God, he thought hastily, Jesus Mary and Joseph forget I said that. (He didn't want her to die. He'd proved that, hadn't he?) Jesus Mary and Joseph (borrowing her saints) forget I said anything. Everything that was exotic and superstitious and despairing in his nature came to the surface, and he stopped walking and stood there, weaving to and fro, pressing his hands together. What he wanted to do was to run away and never come back.

And he could do that. He could leave Anna. He could just drop out of everything and disappear. There were a thousand other streets to live in, and no one would be able to find him. He would be free.

He felt better at once, and it all began to come very clear in his mind. The first thing to do would be to get hold of Ernie. He would tell Ernie to find Anna's mother and make her go to the hospital. Then Anna would go home where she belonged, and everything would be all right. She could even keep the television set if she wanted to—she and her Mama could lie around all day, watching television. She would forget him entirely . . . . .

He jammed his hands into his pockets and breathed hard. His stomach felt like it had a hole in it, but that was because he hadn't eaten since yesterday. What he had to do now was find Ernie, and then he could go eat. He would tell Ernie that Anna had been sick, and he would tell how he had carried her down the stairs and into the street, and how he had held up a car, without a gun or anything, and made the little screeching man take them to the hospital. He would tell how the nurses had come running and how Anna was safe now and was going to be all right and didn't need him any more. After a while, she would get used to the knowing that he had gone forever, and she would find another Mig to protect her.

Jealousy caught him unprepared again and shook him crazily so that he hunched his shoulders against it. He told himself that Anna could never belong to anybody the way she belonged to him. Besides, he had probably saved her life, hadn't he? That ought to give him the right to leave her, if he wanted to. But he felt her holding him with her arms, here, outside, on the street, just as she had held him in the hospital, and he knew that, unless he ran away now, he would never be able to do it. Violently, in his mind, he cast her off.

Someone said his name and he looked up and saw Ernie, staring at him like he was a spook come out of the pavement. "Mig!" Ernie said again. "Where you been?"

The screwed-up faithful little face was a kind of comfort. He could talk to Ernie, if only because Ernie was so stupid. "I been with Anna," Mig said. "She's in the hospital."

The screwed-up face fell apart. "What happened? What'd they do to her?"

Mig said angrily exactly what he had not meant to say, "It wasn't them, it was Mama Kraus," and instantly he wanted the words back. Ernie might be stupid, but it was perfectly plain that Mama Kraus's name had told him all he needed to know.

"She going to die?" said Ernie, very small.

Mig choked back what was close to coming out as a scream. He said "No" very loudly and stared at Ernie hard, but nothing showed in the screwed-up face except relief.

"Little old Anna," Ernie said sentimentally. And then, without warning, slowly, exquisitely, he began to define Mama Kraus. The words fell out of his mouth, searing and precise, like striking snakes. All the words he had ever heard or invented fell on her, and, when his long curse was over at last, there was a peaceful look on his face as if he had been listening to angels.

Mig said "Yeah" gratefully. Mama Kraus lay on the sidewalk between them, pinned down and spreadeagled, her little pig eyes shut forever in her fat face. She would never frighten anyone again, Mig thought, and, having thought that, he finally knew how frightened Anna must have been.

Ernie, with his ritual murder ended, offered Mig the only other talent that he had. "Anything you want me to pick up for Anna?" he said hopefully. "You know, like things she needs?"

"I'll give her anything she needs," Mig said sharply. It was not at all what he had meant to say. He had meant to tell Ernie to find Anna's mother. He had meant to tell Ernie that he was going away. He had meant to tell Ernie to carry to Anna the news that Mig was gone forever. Let her lie there in her white bed and hear that Mig was gone, that Joseph was gone too.

Ernie shuffled his feet apologetically. "Sure, Sure, Mig. I just thought there might be something . . ."

"She don't need nothing. I'll take care of her." He heard his own voice, closing the trap. "I know how to take care of her," he said, and suddenly, eagerly, he began to tell Ernie exactly how well he had taken care of her the night before. Ernie was the perfect audience, and, in the telling, the story grew somewhat. Perhaps not all of it was true (the man in the car had not tried to knock him down, Mig himself had not demanded two doctors in instant attendance), but most of it was. In spite of all the devils and all the fears, he had been able to get Anna to the hospital, and she lay there now, safe and whole, and it was his own doing. He hadn't even needed Ernie. When it had come right down to it, he had been able to manage everything by himself. If he could manage that, he could manage anything.

Jesus Mary and Joseph. Jesus Mary Joseph and Anna, he could manage anything.

He finished his story. Ernie was soaking it up, his eyes were sticking out of his head. Mig said, warningly, "Don't tell nobody about Anna being sick. I'll kill you if you tell." He didn't have to say why he didn't want anybody to know; Ernie knew why already.

After a moment, "Lou?" said Ernie piteously.

"No, not anybody." But he wanted to do something for Ernie, and after a moment, he said reluctantly, "All right, you can tell Lou. But I'll kill her if—"

"Sure, sure," Ernie promised, loyally accepting his orders. "I'll tell Lou that you'll kill her." He giggled. They looked at each other foolishly, both feeling a little drunk, then Ernie said, "Where you heading now?"

He had no idea where he was heading, but he had got this far and the knowledge brought him a dim sense of comfort. He still wanted to run, but he still wasn't running. He answered Ernie's question. "Eat first, and then back to the hospital. There's the Visiting Hours," he explained carefully. "I have to be there."

"See you," said Ernie, impressed.

"See you," said Mig.

37

"I am like to die of grief." I had an old woman say that to me once, and that is how I feel now. I put too much into Mig, I can see that, but seeing it is no comfort. He has run out on me. He has run out on all of us who were trying to help him, and he has taken Anna with him. I will try to tell it clearly, without trumpet flourishes.

(Although I suppose it is a sort of flourish even to announce that there will be none. Well, I will try to do the best I can.)

This afternoon I went to Mig's room, which is what I should have done a week ago and what I had not done because I wanted him to come to me. Today, however, it all seemed very simple and obvious. I felt generous and openhearted and easy. If Mig was not there, Anna would be. And, I thought, Anna likes and trusts me. There would be no problems at all.

I had never been to Mig's room before (a policy) but I know the building very well. Dirty, gritty and mean as it is, it is not one of the worst ones here, although I believe it has been condemned. Apparently no one remembered to pull it down. It has a lobby but no street door, mailboxes with no locks but no mail either, a staircase that has been broken down by rats of all kinds and sexes. I am stupefied by this kind of building, but what do you say about it up here where Hell is not an expletive but a location?

I had no idea what floor Mig would be on, or behind what

door, but I was in luck. On the second floor, a door was half open, and I could see a little man in a suit of baggy underwear. I stuck my head impertinently into his room, and he shrieked—an absolute old maid of an old man—and jittered at me. The law was certainly on his side, I was a trespasser, but the feeling of self-confidence that had brought me this far did not desert me. I asked him, with really exquisite courtesy, whether he knew anyone named Mig.

He said, "Top-floor-he's-gone" as if it was all one word, and then he leaped forward and slammed the door on me. I thought he must be rather a brave person to have answered me at all, because, although I probably don't look like a mugger, who does? Anyway, I liked him and he contributed to my feeling of security.

The old billy-goat must know Mig, I figured, or he would not have known that he was gone. Or he might be wrong. No matter. I could still talk to Anna. I began to climb, and top-floor was a hundred miles away. I was annoyed to find myself a little winded when I got there. There were two doors to choose between, but one of them had a hole kicked clean through it. I chose the other.

No one answered my knock, and after a moment I tried again. When nothing happened, I hammered on the wood, but there is a kind of silence behind a door that means emptiness, and after a while I put down my hand and shook the doorknob. It turned without resistance, and I had a sudden duplicating memory of knocking at Lonergan-Logan's door and of warning myself that I might find him dead. My heart started beating in my throat, and my river of ease drained away. I turned the knob and went in. I don't know what I expected to find. Not what was there.

Rooms can be so empty. There was a bed, unmade, sheet on the floor, no blanket. There was a dress on the floor, a pair of small shoes in one corner. I thought of what small feet Anna had. There was a romantic bad-mad belt, studded with brasshead nails, hanging on a hook. A couple of chairs. A television set. Mig didn't come by that honestly, I thought, my mind already beginning to fit together all the jigsaw pieces it didn't want to know.

There was a table in the middle of the room, some spread-out newspapers. On the floor, next to one of the table legs, was a glassine envelope. It is quite a long while since I have been a baby innocent about anything up here, and, when I found the envelope, I knew that it was what I had expected to find. I picked up one of the newspapers and shook it out, and a few white grains fell down on the dark wood. I licked my finger and touched one of the grains and tasted it. Well, there you are, I told myself calmly, that's what you've been expecting.

I dusted my hands together neatly, and I went over to the television set and turned it on. Nice set, nice clear picture. The housing facilities may not be very good, but the television reception is first-rate. No distortion, no interference. A very pleasant-looking man was holding up a bottle on the screen and assuring me from a clean, full heart that Nature's sunshiny vitamins would give me more pep and more happiness.

I turned the TV off carefully. I didn't need to ask myself where Mig had got the money for it, because I knew. I thought I probably ought to tell Detective Sloan about life on this top floor, but then I thought, icily, What's one more drug-pusher among so many?

And then I leaned over the table and put both hands down on top of the newspaper (I can remember seeing a headline, it was something about the Supreme Court) and I thought maybe I was going to be sick but the feeling passed off.

I left everything just the way I found it, and then I went downstairs and outside into the street and I began to walk. I walked the way people do when their doctors have told them that walking will benefit their health. I walked steadily, earnestly, keeping my mind a careful blank. When I saw Mrs. Detty coming toward me, my mind started to work again and

I turned around and went in the opposite direction. When I saw Irmalee and Cassy, I waved a hand and hurried on. When I thought I saw Detective Sloan, I went and sheltered in a doorway, but it wasn't Detective Sloan at all, just another man with heavy shoulders.

By the time I ran into Ernie, my sickness was turning into anger, and I quite literally collared the poor little scut. His pasty face got pastier, and he disowned any knowledge of Mig so completely that it seemed to me as if he was disowning Mig too. I dropped him distastefully, and I left him shivering on the sidewalk like a puppy. I felt a little guilty, but then I told myself that it was high time that I stopped pampering my conscience, taking all the blame for other people's troubles. Time for Richard to stop Doing Good. Time for Richard to start living his own life.

I thought of going to see Father Bailey, but I rejected the idea savagely and I transferred my anger from Ernie to him. The good clergyman would only pour syrup on my wounds, reassure me that all is for the best in this best of all possible worlds. Mig won the television set in a raffle, no doubt. He is not pushing drugs, but studying to be a pharmacist. He has got a responsible job as night watchman in a bank and has taken Anna with him to carry his lunch box.

Codd thinks I have a great sense of humor. Let's wipe the silly grin off my face and start again. There are no miracles, and Mig is what I have always been afraid he might be. My failure is complete and it is my own fault, because I have made Mig into my touchstone of success. If I take this sheet of paper out of my typewriter now, I will put another sheet in and type a letter of resignation. Dear Father Foundation:

No, I don't think I can do that. I'm entitled to a few more failures, I guess. I failed with my book, and now I have failed with Mig. I had very high hopes for both of them.

The real reason I came back here to this room, instead of

going to Father Bailey, is that I already know what he will say. Or, rather, what he will not say. He will not try to comfort me, he will not preach. He will just sit there and hear me out, a little sad, very kind, and—in the face of all the evidence—persistently hopeful. And I will find myself realizing once more that Father Bailey is indeed a man of faith and that he believes that "too good to be true" really is a blasphemous remark.

I cannot share his faith, but the fact is that I want to. I want to believe that Mig is not vicious, Anna not doomed, even that some day I will write a good book.

I suppose that the real difference between Father Bailey and me is that, so far as I am concerned, Mig's story is now over. Father Bailey will not agree, and it may be that I ought at least to have faith in his faith. Not to turn to the light perhaps, as he always seems able to do, but just not to turn so instinctively to the darkness.

Might that not be a place to start?